SHORT AND SWEET

SHORT AND SWEET

Short texts and how to use them

ALAN MALEY

PENGUIN
ENGLISH

To Leszek Szkutnik, who opened my eyes to the possibilities of short texts

PENGUIN ENGLISH

Published by the Penguin Group
Penguin Books Ltd, 27 Wrights Lane, London W8 5TZ, England
Penguin Books USA Inc., 375 Hudson Street, New York, New York 10014, USA
Penguin Books Australia Ltd, Ringwood, Victoria, Australia
Penguin Books Canada Ltd, 10 Alcorn Avenue, Toronto, Ontario, Canada M4V 3B2
Penguin Books (NZ) Ltd, 182–190 Wairau Road, Auckland 10, New Zealand

Penguin Books Ltd, Registered Offices: Harmondsworth, Middlesex, England

Published by Penguin Books 1993
10 9 8 7 6 5 4 3 2

The moral right of the author and illustrator has been asserted

Illustrations by Clive Collins

Printed and bound in Great Britain by
Butler & Tanner Ltd, Frome and London

Set in Linotron Bembo and Futura by Intype, London

The publishers make grateful acknowledgement to the following for permission to reprint copyright photographs:
page 26 (left) D. Ridgers/Barnaby's, (middle) Val Bissland/Barnaby's, (right) Barnaby's; page 27 (left) Day Williams/Barnaby's, (middle) Jill Chamberlain/Barnaby's, (left) AdLib/Barnaby's; page 88 (left) Day Williams/Barnaby's (middle) AdLib/Barnaby's, (left,) Homer Sykes/ Network.

ACKNOWLEDGEMENTS

The publishers make grateful acknowledgement to the following for permission to reprint copyright material:

AFP, 'Fishy cocktails', *The Independent*, 9 March 1992; AFP, 'Miracle Cure', *The Independent*, 15 April 1992; AFP, 'Pricey dust-ups', *The Independent*, 30 March 1992; Eric Amann, 'a night train passes' and 'quietly dozing', by permission of the author; AP, 'Small victory', *The Independent*, 26 February 1992; Bishop George Appleton, 'Lord, my heart is not large enough', from *The Oxford Book of Prayer* edited by George Appleton, Oxford University Press, 1985; St Francis of Assisi, 'Lord, make me an instrument of your peace', from *St Francis of Assisi Omnibus of Sources: Early Writings and Early Biographies* edited by Marion A. Habig OFM, Franciscan Herald Press, 1973; Winona Baker, 'old cemetery', reprinted from *Beyond the Lighthouse* by Winona Baker by permission of the publisher, Oolichan Books; Frank Barrett, 'Would you credit it?', *The Independent*, 11 April 1992; Bashō, 'a hurried moon' and 'the leeks so white' translated by Cid Corman from Bashō and Shiki from *Born of a Dream* is reprinted by permission of Gnomon Press; Lionel Billows, 'I once had a secretary', 'She was sitting in . . .' and 'Another facility which . . .' by permission of the author; Rabbi Lionel Blue, 'Serious Travel or My Son, the Conference Delegate!' and 'Life is a Moving Staircase', from *Blue Horizons*, Hodder and Stoughton Limited, 1990; Colin Blundell, 'after the earthquake', by permission of the author; Jimmy Boyle, *The Pain of Confinement*, Canongate Press; Vera Brittain, extracts from *Chronicle of Youth: Vera Brittain's War Diary 1913–1917 edited by Alan Bishop* are included with permission of Alan Bishop, Paul Berry, her literary executor and Victor Gollancz Ltd; Walter R. Brooks, 'Ants, Although Admirable Are Awfully Aggravating', from *Collected Poems of Freddy The Pig* by Walter R. Brooks. Copyright 1953 by Walter R. Brooks. Copyright renewed 1981 by Dorothy R. Brooks. Reprinted by permission of Alfred A. Knopf, Inc.; Jack Cain, 'empty room', by permission of the author; John Carden, 'Prayer of a young Ghanaian Christian', from *Morning, Noon and Night*, edited by Rev. John Carden, Church Missionary Society, 1976; John Carden, 'Prayer from Kenya', from *Morning, Noon and Night* edited by Rev. John Carden, Church Missionary Society, 1976; Hugh Casson, *Diary*, Macmillan, by permission of John Johnson Limited; Wendy Cope, 'Flowers', *Serious Concerns*, Faber and Faber Ltd; Noel Coward, *The Noel Coward Diaries*, Weidenfeld and Nicolson; Margaret Cropper, 'God's thought in a man's brain', *Draw Near*, 10 May 1993; *The Daily Mail*, 'Bank heroine walks out on raider', *The Daily Mail*, 4 April 1992, Solo; *The Daily Mail*, 'I was the Loch Ness Monster', *The Daily Mail*, 22 August 1992, Solo; Geoffrey Daniel, 'a thin envelope', reprinted from *The Haiku Hundred* (IRON PRESS 1992); Richard

D'eath, twenty-one epitaphs reprinted from *The Best of Tombstone Humour*, Souvenir Press Ltd; Paul Donovan, 'The Icy Grave' and 'A Grief Observed', © Times Newspapers Ltd, 12 April 1992; Dee Evetts, 'home after dark', reprinted from *The Haiku Hundred* (IRON PRESS 1992); Dee Evetts, 'with a flourish' and 'morning sneeze', by permission of the author; Gavin Ewart, 'Ending', from *Collected Poems 1933–1980* by Gavin Ewart, Hutchinson; Robert Frost, from 'Dust of Snow', *The Poetry of Robert Frost* edited by Edward Connery Lathem, Jonathan Cape; *The Evening Standard*, 'Cheers', *The Evening Standard*, 9 June 1992, Solo; *The Evening Standard*, 'Dustmen find family fortune', *The Evening Standard*, 17 June 1992, Solo; Susan Gill, 'I feel well equipped . . .', *The Independent*, 4 April 1992; Girl Guide Grace reproduced by kind permission of the GGA (UK); E.D. Glover, 'the kingfisher strikes', by permission of the author; Helen Griffiths, 'In sincere praise of older parents', *The Independent*, 4 April 1992; Dag Hammarskjöld translated by W.H. Auden and Leif Sjöberg, 'Night is drawing nigh', from *Markings*, Faber and Faber Ltd; Charles Handy, 'Last Month We Closed a Factory' and 'Group-think', from *Inspirations*, Hutchinson; Brian Harris, 'Listen to the Lions', *The Independent*, 1 November 1992; Cor van den Heuvel, 'hot night' and 'after posting the letter', by permission of the author; Gary Hotham, 'waiting room quiet', 'home early' and 'distant thunder', by permission of the author; *The Independent on Sunday* and *The Independent*, series of extracts from television programme reviews and previews, *The Independent on Sunday* and *The Independent*; *The Independent*, 'Children on aircraft "get a raw deal" ', *The Independent*, 24 February 1992; *The Independent*, 'The Bank of England . . .', *The Independent*, 31 August 1990; Elizabeth Searle-Lamb, 'the old album', from *39 Blossoms* © 1982 by Elizabeth Searle-Lamb, by permission of the author; Peggy Willis Lyles, 'summer night', by permission of the author; Phyliss McGinley, 'The Adversary' *Times Three*, Martin Secker & Warburg; Roger McGough, 'An Apology', *A Holiday on Death Row*. Reprinted by permission of the Peters Fraser & Dunlop Group Ltd; Roger McGough, '40 – Love', from *The Mersey Sound*. Reprinted by permission of the Peters Fraser & Dunlop Group Ltd; Wes Magee, 'Growing up?', from *Morning Break and other poems*, by Wes Magee, Cambridge University Press, 1989; Gerda Mayer, 'Shallow Poem', by permission of the author; Professor John Mbiti, 'A Pygmy hymn', from *Prayers of African Religion*, The Society for the promotion of Christian Knowledge, 1975; Spike Milligan, 'I've never felt finer', by permission of Spike Milligan Productions Ltd; Mini-sagas, *The Book of Mini-sagas*, © Alan Sutton Publishing, *The Sunday Telegraph*, 1985; Mini-sagas, *The Book of Mini-sagas II*, © Alan Sutton Publishing, *The Sunday Telegraph*, 1988; Mike Mitchell, 'Revenge is sweet', *The Independent*, 4 April 1992; Malcolm Muggeridge, *The Diaries*, HarperCollins; Ogden Nash, 'The Purist', from *I'm Stranger Here Myself*, Curtis Brown Ltd. 1938; Dorothy Parker, 'One Perfect Rose', by permission of Duckworth; Frances Partridge, *Everything to Lose: Diaries 1945–60* Victor Gollancz, by permission of Rogers, Coleridge & White Ltd; Veronica Piekosz, 'Stomaching the truth', *The Independent*, 1 May 1992; Peter Popham, 'The Descent of Mam', *The Independent Magazine*, 6 March 1993; Prayer written by an unknown prisoner in Ravensbruck concentration camp was reprinted from

Blessings edited by Mary Craig, Hodder & Stoughton Ltd, 1979; Barbara Pym, *A Very Private Eye*, Macmillan London; Michel Quoist, 'I have just hung up', from *Prayers of Life*, Gill & Macmillan Ltd, 1965; James Reeves, 'Things to Come', © James Reeves. Reprinted by permission of the James Reeves Estate; Reuter, 'Colas banned', *The Independent*, 23 April 1992; Reuter, 'Horse surprise', *The Independent*, 8 April 1992; Theodore Roethke, 'Night Crow', *The Collected Poems of Theodore Roethke*, Faber and Faber Ltd; Emily Romano, 'august heat', by permission of the author; John Godfrey Saxe, 'The Blind Men and the Elephant'; Myra Scovel, 'the silence', first published in *The Haiku Anthology*; Shiki, 'the boat and the shore', translated by Cid Corman from Bashö and Shiki from *Born of a Dream* is reprinted by permission of Gnomon Press; Leon Leszek Szkutnik, twenty-eight mini-texts by permission of the author; W.M. Tidmarsh, 'an old man watches', by permission of the author; Olivia Timbs, 'Not goofy', *The Independent*, 21 April 1992; David A. Walker, 'drought suddenly ends', by permission of the author; Denton Welch, *The Journals*, Alison & Busby, by permission of David Higham Associates; Colin West, 'Misguided Marcus', by permission of the author; Rod Willmot, 'listening', by permission of the author; Annie Wright, 'between the pages', reprinted from *The Haiku Hundred*. (IRON PRESS 1992), by permission of the author; Arizona Zipper, 'I stop to listen', by permission of the author.

Every effort has been made to trace copyright holders in every case. The publishers would be interested to hear from any not acknowledged here.

CONTENTS

INTRODUCTION

This book brings together two simple yet powerful ideas:
- that short, complete texts can be highly productive in foreign-language teaching
- that there is a set of generalizable exercise types which can be applied to virtually any text.

By bringing together a collection of texts with a set of procedures, a very large number of varied language activities can be generated.

Why short texts?

There are many advantages in using short, rather than long, texts:
- Students can read them relatively rapidly and can then get on with the activities with a minimum of delay.
- A larger number and range of texts can be offered in the limited time available.
- When carefully chosen, they use relatively simple language but often contain mature and complex ideas. This offers one way round the problem of students who have a modest level of language competence in English combined with cognitive and affective maturity in their own language.
- Their very concision demands interpretation and expansion, if they are to be fully understood. This work in interpreting texts can focus both on the thinking and the feeling sides of the student's personality. Students are encouraged to relate the text to their own lives and previous experience. Minimal input leads to maximal output.

What are generalizable procedures?

The current multiplicity of language-teaching techniques is potentially confusing for teachers. An attempt has been made here to put these detailed techniques into larger, more generalized groupings each of which is characterized by a key feature.

For example, the category *Reconstruction* requires that a defective or incomplete text be restored to a coherent or complete state. This can be done in all sorts of different ways including jumbled items, gapped texts, reconstruction from a word array, etc. But all of them are examples of the major category of *Reconstruction*.

By organizing materials into generalizable categories it is possible to reduce the bewildering variety of techniques to manageable proportions. On the one hand it offers teachers a check-list for preparing their own materials. On the other it gives them a tool for evaluating existing published materials.

How is the book organized?

Part 1: Twelve generalizable procedures

Here the categories are described and examples given of the exercise types which may be included within each of them.

This part is intended as a ready-reference for teachers wishing to prepare lessons based on the texts in Part 2. Having selected a text to work with, the teacher should find it useful to check back to Part 1 to see which procedures might most profitably be used with it.

Part 2: The texts

There is a division into sections based on text-types, ranging from one-line texts such as proverbs up to two-page essays. The full list can be found in the Table of Contents. There is a rough progression from shorter to slightly longer texts as the book advances.

Each section begins with a fully worked example. The remainder of the section is taken up with texts only. Having worked through the example, it should be clear how the other texts might be approached.

How should the book be used?

It is clearly *not* intended as a course book to be followed from beginning to end.

For teachers it should fulfil two functions:
• to offer a set of varied language practice material on which to base some of their teaching
• to encourage them to develop the ideas further on texts they select themselves.

In class, the activities work best if done in pairs or small groups with plenty of scope for interaction.

Some teachers may wish to use the texts as home-study materials for certain groups of students. They could also be used in self-study mode in Self-access Study Centres.

A note on the sample texts

The sample texts are intended to serve as examples. They do not exhaust the possibilities for developing language work based on the texts. Individual teachers will doubtless find other ways of using them. They should, however, help in getting started.

It should be obvious that no teacher would wade his or her way through *all* the exercises suggested but would make a judicious selection. The exercises can also be done in a different order.

The rubrics are addressed directly to the student. They would need to be modified to suit the level of different groups.

There are additionally some activities which can be carried out on all the texts in a section. Students can be asked to look back over the whole section and *select* (or *rank*) texts as being most suitable for given purposes.

e.g. • Select the text you would most like to send to someone you are worried about.
   • Which text would be most suitable as advertising copy?
   • Which text would you find it easiest to translate?
   • Which three texts do you like most? Put them in order and explain why.
   • Which three do you like least? Put them in order and explain why.

Some students may also like to commit some of the texts to memory. Others may like to build up a file index or scrapbook of texts on a given theme.

PART 1

TWELVE GENERALIZABLE PROCEDURES
and CLASSROOM PROCEDURES

Each major category will be described. Examples of possible activities will then be given.

Although most of the procedures can be applied to most of the texts, they *need not all be used*. There is no point in wringing the text dry just for the sake of completeness. It is also often the case that a given text works better with certain procedures than with others. The detailed permutation of procedures and texts is in any case a decision only the teacher can properly make.

1 EXPANSION
Key criterion: the text must be lengthened in some way.
Examples
- Add one or more sentences/paragraphs to the beginning and end of the text.
- Add specified items within the text (e.g. adjectives).
- Add sentences within the text.
- Add subordinate clauses within the text.
- Add comment within the text.

2 REDUCTION
Key criterion: the text must be shortened in some way.
Examples
- Remove specified items (e.g. adjectives).
- Turn it into telegraphese.
- Combine sentences.
- Remove clauses/sentences.
- Rewrite in a different format.
(See also **3** Media transfer and **8** Reformulation, below.)

3 MEDIA TRANSFER
Key criterion: the text must be transferred into a different medium or format.
Examples
- Transfer it into visual form (e.g. pictures, graphs, maps, tables etc.).
- Turn prose into poem (or vice versa).

- Turn a letter into a newspaper article (or vice versa).
- Turn a headline into a proverb (or vice versa).
- Turn a poem into an advertising slogan (or vice versa).
- Turn a prose narrative into a screenplay.

4 MATCHING
Key criterion: a correspondence must be found between the text and something else.
Examples
- Match text with a visual representation.
- Match text with a title.
- Match text with another text.
- Match text with a voice/music.

5 SELECTION/RANKING
Key criterion: the text must be chosen according to some given criterion. (In the case of Ranking, several texts must be placed in order of suitability for a given criterion.)
Examples
- Choose the best text for a given purpose (e.g. inclusion in a teenage magazine).
- Choose the most/least (difficult, formal, personal, complex . . .) text.
- Choose the text most/least like the original version.
- Choose words from a text to act as an appropriate title.

6 COMPARISON/CONTRAST
Key criterion: points of similarity/difference must be identified between two or more texts.
Examples
- Identify words/expressions common to both texts.
- Identify words/phrases in one text which are paraphrased in the other.
- Identify ideas common to both texts.
- Identify facts present in one text and not in the other.
- Compare grammatical/lexical complexity. (See also II (p.6), Analysis.)

7 RECONSTRUCTION
Key criterion: coherence/completeness must be restored to an incomplete or defective text.

Examples
- Insert appropriate words/phrases into gapped texts.
- Reorder jumbled words, lines, sentences, paragraphs etc.
- Reconstruct sentences/texts from a word array.
- Reconstitute a written text from an oral presentation. (various types of dictation)
- Remove sentences/lines which do not 'belong' in the text.

8 REFORMULATION
Key criterion: the text must be expressed in a form different from the original without loss of essential meanings.
Examples
- Retell a story from notes/memory.
- Use keywords to rewrite a text.
- Rewrite in a different format. (e.g. prose as poem) (See also **3** above, Media transfer.)
- Rewrite in a different style/mood.

9 INTERPRETATION
Key criterion: personal knowledge/experience must be used to clarify and extend the meaning(s) of the text.
Examples
- What does this recall from your own experience?
- What does this remind you of?
- What images does this throw up?
- What associations does it have?
- What questions would you wish to ask the author?
- Formulate questions on the text beginning: what?, who?, where?, when?, why?, how? . . .
- Is the text true/likely?
- What does the text *not* say that it might have said?

10 CREATING TEXT
Key criterion: the text is to be used as a springboard for the creation of new texts.
Examples
- Write a parallel text on a different theme.
- Use the same story outline/model to write a new text.
- Quarry words from text A to create a new text B.
- Use the same title but write a new text.
- Add lines/sentences to the text to reshape it. (See also **1** Expansion and **8** Reformulation, above.)
- Combine these texts to create a new text.

11 ANALYSIS

Key criterion: the text is to be submitted to some form of language-focused scrutiny.

Examples

- Work out the ratio of one-word verbs to two word verbs.
- How many different tenses are used? Which are most/least frequent?
- How many content (or function) words does the text contain?
- List the different ways in which the word X is referred to in the text. (anaphoric reference)
- List all the words to do with (the sea, movement, ecology etc.) in this text.

12 PROJECT WORK

Key criterion: the text is used as a springboard for some related practical work with a concrete outcome.

Examples

- Use the text as the centrepiece of an advertising campaign. First decide on the product. Then design the campaign posters, advertising jingles etc. Finally present the product as a TV commercial (which must incorporate the text). If possible video it.
- This text is about the problem of X. Design a questionnaire on this problem for other groups to complete. Tabulate the results and present them to the rest of the class.
- This text presents a particular point of view. With a partner, prepare a brief magazine article which either supports or disagrees with this point of view. In both cases you will need to collect ideas and examples to support your own point of view. Display the articles on the class notice-board.

CLASSROOM PROCEDURES

Unless otherwise indicated, the normal procedure to adopt with all the suggested activities is:

1 *Individual work* Each student first does the activity for her/himself. This ensures that everyone makes an initial personal effort.
2 *Pair work* (or work in threes) Students work together to compare and discuss what they have produced individually.
3 *Class work* The pair work then feeds back into whole-class discussion as appropriate.

There are a few cases when *group work* is preferable to pair work, especially in 12 Project work. This is always clearly indicated.

Normally the group work would also be rounded off in a whole-class feedback session.

NB These procedures are recommended for any activity you choose. This does not mean you have to do *all* the activities.

PART 2

THE TEXTS

This section contains different types of text, usually not longer than one line: proverbs, word definitions and book and film titles.

Because they are so short, they usually have a lot of meaning packed tightly into them. This meaning can be 'unpacked' in various ways through the exercises.

The Sample Text: Eat the grape and not the vine. (Turkish proverb)

1 EXPANSION
a) Insert a phrase or clause before the proverb.
   e.g. • *Wise people* eat the grape and not the vine.
   • *We should all learn to* eat the grape and not the vine.
   • *It is better to learn to* eat the grape and not the vine.
b) Add a clause beginning with 'otherwise' after the proverb.
   e.g. Eat the grape and not the vine, *otherwise you will go hungry next year/you'll starve/you'll regret it* etc.
c) Imagine this proverb is the last sentence of a short story. Write the story which leads up to the proverb.
   e.g. There once was a man who lived in a beautiful forest. He used the dead wood which fell from the trees as firewood and there was always enough. Then one day a man came from the city and offered him a lot of money for the forest. The man sold it to him. Within a month all the trees had been cut down. Now the man had no firewood and the rain washed away the soil in his fields. He had to spend all his money to buy food and fuel. He should have remembered the old Turkish proverb 'Eat the grape and not the vine'.

2 REDUCTION
a) Make the proverb shorter by starting it with 'Don't'.
   e.g. Don't eat vines, eat grapes.
b) Shorten it to four words by making the nouns into plurals.
   e.g. Eat grapes, not vines.

3 MEDIA TRANSFER
a) Write a newspaper headline based on the proverb.

e.g. • Minister's Plea: Eat Grapes, Conserve Vines
   • New Agricultural Policy – Grapes not Vines
   • Save our Vines, Eat Grapes Say Farmers

b) Write an advertising slogan based on the proverb.
   e.g. You eat the grapes. We'll take care of the vines.
      Vines are our business. Grapes are yours.

4 MATCHING

Here are several other proverbs. Which one(s) match the meaning
of 'Eat the grape and not the vine'?
• Waste not, want not.
• While the grass grows, the horse starves.
• Don't kill the goose that lays the golden eggs.
• Only a mad dog eats its own tail.
• If heaven throws you a plum, open your mouth.

5 SELECTION/RANKING

a) Here are a series of topics. To which one would the proverb serve
   as the most appropriate title?
   • Healthy diet
   • Nature conservation
   • Wine-making
   • Agricultural policy
   • Home economics

b) Here are several proverbs. Put them in order from most like to
   least like the original proverb.
   • Spare the rod and spoil the child.
   • Eat the egg and not the chicken.
   • Great oaks from little acorns grow.
   • Live today and pay tomorrow.
   • Look after the pence and the pounds will look after themselves.
   • The proof of the pudding is in the eating.

6 COMPARISON/CONTRAST

a) Look up the third Nasruddin story on p. 112 (about the boiled
   eggs). What similarities can you find between the story and this
   proverb? What differences are there?

b) What is the difference in meaning between the Turkish proverb
   and these?
   • Make hay while the sun shines.
   • Time and tide wait for no man.
   • Tomorrow will take care of itself.

7 RECONSTRUCTION

a) These words can be used to make up a proverb. Try to make as many versions as you can:

grape   not   the   vine   eat   and

e.g. • Eat the grape and the vine; not the vine and the grape.
   • The vine and the grape eat not.
   • Eat the grape and not the vine.
   • Eat the vine and not the grape.

b) Choose the words from below which best fill the gaps in this proverb.

Eat the _____ and not the _____.

forest bush trees vine grass field grape cherry leaf

8 REFORMULATION

a) Rewrite the proverb in a way that makes its meaning clear.

e.g. • If you want to have grapes from your vine next year, don't eat the vine this year, only the grapes.
   • It's all right to eat the grapes but make sure you don't destroy the vine, otherwise there will be no grapes next year.

b) Rewrite the proverb as a short poem or as a haiku (see p. 18).

e.g. each year the grape comes
   enjoy it to the full – but
   don't destroy the vine

9 INTERPRETATION

a) Read the proverb with a partner. Discuss what you think it really means. Try to write out your interpretation. Then compare it with another pair.

e.g. It means that if we don't look after renewable resources we will have no future.

b) Can you think of an incident from your own experience which the proverb illustrates?

10 CREATING TEXT

a) Write a parallel proverb with the same or a similar meaning to this one.

e.g. • Cut the rose but leave the bush.
   • This year's corn is next year's seed.
   • Cut one tree – plant two.

b) Brainstorm as many proverbs or sayings in English as you can. (Use those listed on the following pages, too.) Then choose up to six of them and arrange them in an order which makes a kind of poem. You can add connecting words if you wish.

II ANALYSIS

a) What is the grammatical form of the proverb? (interrogative? imperative? indicative?) Look at all the other proverbs in this section. How many have the same form? What other characteristic forms do proverbs have? (e.g. If . . .)

b) Why does the proverb use 'the' (the grape, the vine) rather than 'a' or the plural (grapes, vines)?

12 PROJECT WORK

a) In a group, collect English (or non-English) proverbs which have common characteristics.

e.g. They are all in the imperative form (injunctions):
   • Look before you leap.
   • Waste not, want not.
   • Take care of the pence and the pounds will take care of themselves etc.

Or they all include references to food, or to money, or to animals etc. Prepare a display for the class notice-board.

b) In groups, prepare a visual display with pictures, labels and short texts to show how the earth's resources are being destroyed. The title for the display will be 'Eat the grape and not the vine'.

Some further ideas

Before selecting a single text to work on you may find it helpful to set up one or two tasks which involve reading through all the material here. For example:

a) Look through all the proverbs and group them according to criteria which you decide on, e.g. all those which refer to items of food, all those expressed as imperatives, all those which refer to people etc.

b) Look through the titles. Choose up to six which seem to 'belong together', then write them out as a kind of poem. For example:

   i) Land of Silence and Darkness
       Too Loud a Solitude
       Distant Voices: Still Lives
       The Silence of the Lambs
       Scream of Stone
   ii) The Angel of Pain

Scream of Stone
A Good Looking Corpse
The Flesh and the Fiend
Shoot the Women First
The Silence of the Lambs

With very short texts such as these the activities which work best are:

1 Expansion, 3 Media transfer, 4 Matching, 9 Interpretation, 12 Project work.

Proverbs

Waste not, want not.
All that glitters is not gold.
Nothing ventured nothing gained.
The pot calls the kettle black.
Don't put all your eggs in one basket.
Two's company, three's a crowd.
When the cat's away, the mice will play.
A rolling stone gathers no moss.
The grass is always greener on the other side of the fence.
A stitch in time, saves nine.
Strike while the iron is hot.
Money is the hatchet to chop friendship.
If you believe, it's a god; if you don't, it's a stone. (Indian)
The best mirror does not reflect the other side of things. (Japanese)
A healthy man does not seek a doctor. (African)
If heaven throws you a plum, open your mouth. (Chinese)
Buy the neighbour before you buy the house. (Arab)
The absent are always wrong. (French)
A branch that falls in the river does not become a fish. (African)
Only in flight does one know the bird. (Russian)
When two elephants fight, the grass suffers. (African)
If my shoe is tight, who cares if the world is vast? (Turkish)
The only free cheese is in the mousetrap. (Russian)
The girl who can't dance says the band can't play. (Yiddish)
If God lived in the world, people would break his windows.
   (Yiddish)
'For example' is not proof. (Yiddish)
Never whisper to the deaf or wink at the blind. (Slovenian)
Protest long enough that you are right, and you will be wrong.
   (Yiddish)

When a poor man eats a chicken, one or the other is sick. (Yiddish)
He who can lick, can bite. (French)
One chops wood. The other does the grunting. (Russian)
While the grass grows, the horse starves. (Russian)
A stick has two ends. (Russian)

Devil's dictionary

acquaintance, n. A person whom we know well enough to borrow
from, but not well enough to lend to.
bore, n. A person who talks when you wish him to listen.
connoisseur, n. A specialist who knows everything about something and nothing about anything else.
diplomacy, n. The patriotic art of lying for one's country.
erudition, n. Dust shaken out of a book into an empty skull.
immigrant, n. An unenlightened person who thinks one country
better than another.
linguist, n. A person more learned in the languages of others than
wise in his own.
regret, n. The sediment in the cup of life.
relief, n. Waking up early on a cold morning to find that it's Sunday.
revolution, n. In politics, an abrupt change in the form of mis-
government.
saint, n. A dead sinner revised and edited.

Book and film titles

Books

A Closed Eye
The Last Shot
The Old Man and the Sea
Follow the Wind
The Meal a Mile Long
From the House of War
The House that Caught a Cold
Sky Full of Babies
The Dog with the Awful Laugh
Brief Lives
A Good Looking Corpse
City of the Mind

The Angel of Pain
The Secret Mind
The Secret Garden
A Wild Sheep Chase
Tender is the Night
Lonely Hearts of the Cosmos
Shoot the Women First
The Inn at the Edge of the
    World
Darkness Falls from the Air
Howling at the Moon
The Architecture of Desire

The Lady or the Tiger
I am Right: You are Wrong
The Emperor's New Mind
The Eighth Day of the Week
Too Loud a Solitude

Films

Stealing Altitude
A Place in the Sun
Scream of Stone
Where the Green Ants Dream

Land of Silence and Darkness
Heart of Glass
Odd Man Out
Ladder of Swords
Distant Voices: Still Lives
The Silence of the Lambs
Dances with Wolves
The Realm of the Senses
Tree of Hands
The Army in the Shadows
The Flesh and the Fiend
The African Queen

A haiku is a Japanese verse-form based on syllables. It usually has three lines of 5, 7 and 5 syllables each. The object of a haiku is to capture the special quality of particular experiences in a very concrete way.

Haiku are now a very popular verse-form in the West too. Not all Western haiku writers stick to the 5–7–5 rule, however.

The Sample Text:

feet in the river,
eating cool plums on the stones –
now the long climb back

A.M.

1 EXPANSION

a) This haiku does not use full sentences. They are abbreviated. Try to expand the haiku using full sentences.

e.g. We are sitting with our feet in the river, eating cool plums on the stones.

As we do so we are thinking about the long climb back up the hill we came down earlier.

b) Add as many adjectives to the nouns in the haiku as you can.

e.g. sore, dusty, weary feet
cold, clear, deep, fast-running river
flat, hard, rough, wet stones
long, steep, hard, rough climb

c) Write out a description of a day out based on the haiku in three paragraphs. In paragraph one, begin 'We started out early in the morning . . .'

Paragraph two will contain the information from the haiku, e.g. 'Finally we got to the river. What a relief it was to plunge our feet into it . . .'

Paragraph three will describe the climb back to the starting-point.

2 REDUCTION

a) Cut out all the adjectives. Does it change the 'feel' of the haiku?

b) Reduce the haiku to an even more minimal poem, concentrating on keywords and phrases only.

e.g. feet in river
cool plums
now the climb

3 MEDIA TRANSFER

a) Write out the incident described in the haiku as a postcard.

e.g. Dear Tom – had a lovely walk yesterday – down through woods to the river. Ate deliciously cold plums and dangled feet in the water. But the climb back was mighty steep! Best wishes, Emma.

b) Use the haiku as part of an advertisement:

e.g. feet in the river,
eating cool plums on the stones –
now the long climb back
all recorded for your album on Bril-film, the new ultra high-definition film.

4 MATCHING

a) Match the haiku with the title you think fits it best:
  • Summer Afternoon
  • The Heat of the Day
  • Weariness
  • Apprehension

b) Look through the other haiku in this section and try to find another one which matches the mood of the original.

5 SELECTION/RANKING

a) Choose a title for the haiku from among the words that make it up.

e.g. • Cool Feet
      • Eating Plums

b) The haiku might possibly be used for a number of purposes. Put the purposes below in order from most to least likely.
  • as a caption for an art photography book
  • as a text in a tourist brochure
  • as part of an advertisement for climbing-boots
  • as part of a cigarette advertisement

6 COMPARISON/CONTRAST

Here are three haiku versions of the same event:

- feet in the river,
  eating cool plums on the stones –
  now the long climb back
- cold river water,
  stolen plums, quenching our thirst
  the climb steep ahead
- feet in the cold stream
  black plums cool in our dry throats
  the climb in our minds

Compare the three texts in as many ways as you can: which ideas/images are common/different? Which words are identical/similar/different? Which version is the most different from the original? Which new ideas or images are introduced? Which do you prefer?

7 RECONSTRUCTION

a) Use this word array to generate as many sentences as you can. (You can only use the words in the array and no others – but you can use them as many times as you like.)

    river   in   now   plums   on
    the   climb   feet   long   now
    cool   stones   eating   back

e.g. eating plums on the river
    the climb on cool stones
    in the river, cool plums
    the long river, the cool stones, the plums
    the climb etc.

Then choose three of your lines to make a short poem.

b) The lines in this poem have been mixed up. There are also three lines which do not fit. Rewrite the original poem by cutting out three lines and putting the remaining three into what you think is the best order.

    hands in the long summer grass
    now the long climb back
    watching the small fish
    feet in the river,
    time to relax now
    eating cool plums on the stones

8 REFORMULATION

a) Rewrite your own version of the event using these keywords: feet, plums, river, climb.

b) Rewrite the event as an entry in your diary.

c) Rewrite the event as it might have appeared in a spy novel.

9 INTERPRETATION

a) Does this remind you of a similar experience you have had? Make some notes about it. Then use them to tell your partner.

b) Apply the questions who? where? when? why? and how? to the haiku. Use the answers to build up a full picture of the event with your partner.

10 CREATING TEXT

a) There is another Japanese verse-form, called a *tanka*. This follows the haiku form for the first three lines (5–7–5 syllables). It then adds two lines, each of 7 syllables.

Try to transform the haiku into a tanka by adding two lines of 7 syllables.

e.g. feet in the river,
   eating cool plums on the stones –
   now the long climb back
   how far it seems from down here!
   did we really come so far?

b) Write your own haiku version of a similar event.

e.g. top of the mountain
   flasks of hot tomato soup
   how far down it is!

11 ANALYSIS

a) The first two lines could be ambiguous (are the feet eating the plums?). But of course we understand what is meant even though words are missing. Supply the missing words so that the message is clear and unambiguous.

e.g. With our feet in the river, we are eating . . . Now we are thinking about the big climb . . .

When words are left out like this, as they often are in everyday speech and in poems, we call it *ellipsis*.

b) The haiku tells us some things and lets us deduce others. Make a list of the things we know because we are told and those we know because we have worked them out.

e.g.

Told (certain)	*Worked out* (probable)

Told (certain)
- there are feet
- the feet are in the river
- there are plums
- the plums are cool
- someone is eating them etc.

Worked out (probable)
- it is probably summertime
- the feet belong to the writer
- they are probably tired feet
- the person (or people) is probably sitting down
- he/she/they have probably walked a long way already
- earlier the writer had come down from a higher place etc.

What we deduce are often called *inferences*.

12 PROJECT WORK

In groups, try to find out as much as you can about *syllabic* poetry (e.g. haiku, senryu, tanka, quatrains, cinquains etc.). Make a collection of examples of all the types you find. Then prepare a display for the class notice-board.

Some further ideas

In order to become familiar with all the texts, before selecting one for intensive treatment, it may be helpful to set up some tasks which involve comparison and grouping. For example:

a) Put the haiku into groups according to similarities you decide upon.

   e.g. all those to do with age, with seasons of the year, with the weather, with water, with sounds etc.

b) Choose the haiku which has the happiest feeling, and the one which is saddest.

c) Choose the one you would like to have on your desk as a kind of motto.

The activities which tend to work most easily with haiku are:

1 Expansion, 3 Media transfer, 4 Matching, 6 Comparison/contrast, 8 Reformulation, 9 Interpretation, 10 Creating text.

Haiku

old cemetery
all the sprinklers going
in the pouring rain
   Winona Baker

a hurried moon
treetops fastened by
rain
   Bashō, trans. Corman

a thin envelope
on the mat; my name in black
how cold the hallway!
  Geoffrey Daniel

between the pages
of a favourite book I find
squashed fruit-cake crumbs
  Annie Wright

an old man watches
chestnut buds unfurl and sniffs
leafsmoke on the wind
  W.M. Tidmarsh

after the earthquake
some geezer in stone still stands
upright in the square
  Colin Blundell

with a flourish
the waitress leaves behind
rearranged smears
  Dee Evetts

empty room:
one swinging coat hanger
measures the silence
  Jack Cain

the leeks so white
from having just been washed
coldness itself
  Bashō, trans. Corman

quietly dozing
under a clock without hands:
the museum keeper
  Eric Amann

home after dark
through the window my family
of strangers
  Dee Evetts

the kingfisher strikes:
a thousand silver minnow
splinter the stream with light
  Edward Glover

waiting in darkness
an aged blind man sitting . . .
listening for the moon
  R. Christopher Thorsen

drought suddenly ends –
in the brimful water butt
a drowned sparrow
  David A. Walker

morning sneeze –
the guitar in the corner
resonates
  Dee Evetts

autumn wind –
mountain's shadow
wavers
  Issa

the boat and the shore
conversing all day long in
terms of the water
  Shiki, trans. Corman

a night train passes:
pictures of the dead are trembling
  on the mantelpiece
  Eric Amann

distant thunder
the dog's toenails click
against the linoleum
    Gary Hotham

home early –
your empty coat hanger
in the closet
    Gary Hotham

summer night:
we turn out all the lights
to hear the rain
    Peggy Willis Lyles

the silence
while the gift
is being opened
    Myra Scovel

after posting the letter
staring at the slot –
winter rain
    Cor van den Heuvel

I stop to listen;
the cricket
has done the same
    Arizona Zipper

early morning mist
up to the valley's high lip –
sun – trees show their teeth
    Alan Maley

waiting room quiet
an apple core
in the ashtray
    Gary Hotham

the old album:
not recognizing at first
my own young face
    Elizabeth Searle-Lamb

august heat;
the coolness of eggs
in a blue crock
    Emily Romano

hot night
turning the pillow
to the cool side
    Cor van den Heuvel

listening . . .
after a while,
I take up my axe again
    Rod Willmot

small blue butterfly
alights, beats its wings twice –
  soars
dissolves in the sky
    Alan Maley

skeins of early mist
snagged in the trees' high
  branches
the river below
    Alan Maley

All the texts in this section were written by Leszek Szkutnik, a well-known textbook writer in Poland.

They are all in fairly simple language but the feelings and ideas they express are often intense and profound.

They are as important for what they do not say as for what they do. The student is therefore drawn into filling in, from his own experience, what is not stated but only hinted at by the text.

The Sample Text:

He never sent me flowers. He never wrote me letters. He never took me to restaurants. He never spoke of love. We met in parks. I don't remember what he said, but I remember how he said it. Most of it was silence anyway.

I EXPANSION

a) Add as many adjectives as you can to the text.

e.g. He never sent me *beautiful* flowers. He never wrote me *long, passionate* letters. He never took me to *expensive, foreign* restaurants . . .

b) Add some other sentences after '. . . restaurants'. They should tell of the other things 'he' never did.

e.g. He never phoned me. He never gave me presents. He never invited me to his home etc.

c) Add one paragraph before and one paragraph after this text. The first should begin 'It all began . . .' The last should begin 'It ended one day when . . .'

2 REDUCTION

Shorten the text by cutting out repetition.

e.g. He never sent me flowers, wrote me letters, took me to restaurants or spoke of love . . . I don't remember what he said, only how he said it . . .

3 MEDIA TRANSFER

a) Write out the text as a poem. Use the exact words of the text but

arrange them on the page to make the most effect. Give the poem
a title.

e.g. *Heartbreak*

> He never sent me flowers.
> He never wrote me letters.
> He never took me to restaurants.
> He never spoke of love.
>
> We met in parks.
> I don't remember
> What he said,
> But I remember
> How he said it.
>
> Most of it was –
> Silence
> Anyway.

b) Write a letter to the 'agony aunt's' column of a newspaper based
on this text. The letter is asking for advice.

4 MATCHING

a) Here are photographs of three women. Which one do you think
is most likely to have spoken the text?

b) There are photographs of three men on page 26. Which one do you think was the 'he' in the text?

c) Are there any other texts in this section which are on a similar theme?

5 SELECTION

a) Which title best fits the text?

Silence Indifference Anguish Memories Frustration Never

b) Select three words from the text which sum up its meaning for you.

e.g. never love silence

Compare your choice with others.

6 COMPARISON/CONTRAST

Here are two poems on a similar theme:

One Perfect Rose

A single flow'r he sent me, since we met.
  All tenderly his messenger he chose;
Deep-hearted, pure, with scented dew still wet –
  One perfect rose.

I knew the language of the floweret;
  'My fragile leaves,' it said, 'his heart enclose.'
Love long has taken for his amulet
  One perfect rose.

Why is it no one ever sent me yet
  One perfect limousine, do you suppose?
Ah no, it's always just my luck to get
  One perfect rose.
    Dorothy Parker

Flowers

Some men never think of it.
You did. You'd come along
And say you'd nearly brought me flowers
But something had gone wrong.

The shop was closed. Or you had doubts –
The sort that minds like ours

Dream up incessantly. You thought
I might not want your flowers.

It made me smile and hug you then.
Now I can only smile.
But, look, the flowers you nearly brought
Have lasted all this while.
  Wendy Cope

Are there any words in the original which occur in these texts?
Are the ideas the same or different? Is the attitude/mood of the
writer the same in all three texts?

7 RECONSTRUCTION

a) Look at this word array:

silence	was	he
never	love	of
sent	letters	I
took	met	anyway
me	don't	spoke
restaurants	flowers	wrote
parks	said	to
what	how	remember
we	it	in
most		

Make as many sentences as you can using these words only (and
no others). You can use the words as many times as you like.
Then combine your list of sentences with your partner's. Use
some of your sentences to write a short story.

b) These sentences are jumbled up. Try to put them into an order
which makes sense for you.

> We met in parks. He never took me to restaurants. Most of it
> was silence anyway. He never sent me flowers. He never wrote
> me letters. I don't remember what he said, but remember how
> he said it. He never spoke of love.

Then look at the text your teacher will give you. Are there any
differences between the text and your version?

8 REFORMULATION

a) Listen to the text once. Then use these keywords to rewrite it in
your own words.

> flowers parks silence remember never restaurants
> letters love

Then compare your version with the original.

b) Rewrite the text replacing the verbs with possible alternatives.

e.g. He never *brought* me flowers. He never *sent* me letters. He never *invited* me to restaurants. He never *talked about* love. We *walked* in parks. I don't *recall* what he *talked about*, but I recall how he *talked*. Most of it was silence anyway.

c) Rewrite the text using more general language to replace the specific examples.

e.g. He never did any of the things lovers usually do. We met in public places. Most of the time he was silent but I still remember his voice.

9 INTERPRETATION

a) Do you know anyone who has had an unhappy love affair? Was it similar or different to this one?

b) Have you seen the film *Brief Encounter*? How similar is it to the text?

c) Read the text, then close your eyes. What colours does the text suggest to you? Discuss them with your group.

d) What questions would you want to ask the man described in the text? And the woman?

10 CREATING TEXT

a) Imagine that the couple in the text have a final argument before they break up. With your partner write the dialogue they might have spoken.

b) Write a minimal poem using some of the words from the text (not more than ten *different* words). Give it a title.

e.g. *Care-ful Love*
Never flowers.
Never letters.
Never restaurants.
Never love.
I remember –
Silence.

11 ANALYSIS

a) How many tenses are used in the text? Which? What does this tell you about the events which are described?

b) What is the subject of the first four sentences? Of the fifth sentence? Of the sixth sentence? Of the last sentence? Can you see a pattern?

12 PROJECT WORK

In groups of six, design questionnaires to discover what people's attitudes are to courtship. (It might, for example, contain questions relating to what the man should do to attract a partner and what the woman should do.) Then distribute it to the rest of the group to complete. When completing it the men should write (M) at the top and the women (F). When you have collected the results tabulate them in two separate displays: one showing women's attitudes and the other showing men's. One member of the group should prepare a brief talk explaining the results to the rest of the class, using the tabulated results as illustrations.

Some further ideas

It will help to familiarize students with all the texts before you select particular texts for individual treatment. Here are some activities which will help with the process:

a) Look through all the texts in this section and choose the one you would like to send to a very good friend, perhaps on a greeting card.

b) Try to find texts which could be joined together (two or three at a time) and still make sense.

   e.g. The Holiday is Over and Never Again

       You Came and Return

       She Waited and A Very Important Man

The activities which tend to work best with the mini-texts are:

  1 Expansion, 3 Media transfer, 6 Comparison/contrast, 7 Reconstruction, 8 Reformulation, 9 Interpretation.

Mini-texts

1 Yes or no? Here or there? Now or later? It's all up to you. I accept everything without reservation. I'm very tired indeed. Too tired to argue.

2 A letter for him. A picture postcard for her. A message for them. Nothing for me. Not a word from you. An old photograph of us on my desk.

3 *They mean well*

  They are good people. Almost all of them. They may not see

you. They may not help you. They may not understand you. But they are good. They mean well.

4 *The holiday is over*
Our holiday is almost over. We are leaving tomorrow. The weather is perfect. Everything is perfect. Except that the holiday is nearly over. The last day is always the most difficult. It is like death.

5 *They were polite and cold*
I went. I spoke to them. They were polite and cold. They didn't understand. They promised to try again.

6 *You came*
You came. You were late. As usual. But you came. It was a rainy day. But you came. And sunshine filled the world. And music filled the world. Though it was raining. And grey.

7 *Never again*
It's senseless. It's useless. I agree with you. We mustn't meet again. It's as simple as that – never again. By the way, where shall we dine tonight?

8 When the door has closed behind the last visitor, when the attendants have left, what happens to the pictures? How do they exist without being looked at? How do they survive till the first look of recognition?

9 *A good man*
Some people think that I am good. Because I haven't killed anyone. Because I haven't stolen anything. Because I haven't done anything really wrong. Because I haven't had the opportunity.

10 *Return*
It's nice to see you again. I'm so glad you've been able to come. I hope you had a nice journey. You haven't changed at all through all these years. And as you see, nothing has changed here. Your room is exactly as it was on the day when you left. Twenty-four years, seven months, and three days ago.

11 *Taboo*
It's taboo. It's never discussed. It's never even mentioned. It's

accepted as non-existent. But all the time it's at the back of everybody's mind.

12 *She waited*
She waited. She refused to live. She waited for the great event. She waited for years. She never lost faith. She never lost patience. And it came one day. Twenty years too late.

13 *A great temptation*
To phone you. It's a great temptation. To think that you'll lift the receiver and say, 'I've just been thinking about you.' 'I've been waiting for you to phone.' Or some such thing. It's a great temptation to imagine that we can exchange remarks about telepathy. A temptation so great that I dial your number. I dial it. I wait. I forget that you are not there to answer it.

14 *A very important man*
He thought he knew life. He accepted the rules. He was ambitious. To get on in the world. That was what really mattered. He made sacrifices. Tomorrow became more important than today. He slowly killed today. But in the end he succeeded. He succeeded in becoming a very important old man at forty.

15 Life was an ordeal while you were there and yet I managed to live. Life was just miserable while you were away and yet I managed somehow. How will I manage now that you are back? Incidentally, how long are you going to stay?

16 Every civilized person stands in front of a mirror every morning and brushes his teeth. Every civilized person sees the same face in the mirror every morning – his own face. The same face – at seven, at twenty-seven, at seventy-two. The same face, though not always the same teeth.

17 This is an old family photograph. The boy in the middle is me. The two girls are my sisters: the one wearing a hat is Brenda. She died two years ago at the age of seventy-two. The other one is Ann. She died last year at the age of eighty-one. Would you have recognized me in that photograph if I hadn't told you it was me?

18 *I lack imagination*
I ought to have written. I should have phoned. I ought to have

let you know I was coming. I know that I placed you in a very awkward position. And it's all because I lack imagination. It simply never occurred to me that there might be another person involved. Of course I don't have to tell you how frightfully sorry I am.

19 *Why?*
Apart from everything else, it's interesting psychologically. Why did he do it? He was quite healthy, wasn't he? I mean physically. Perhaps not mentally. He can't have been quite normal, I agree. To do a thing like that at forty. If he had been twenty . . . Then perhaps . . . At any rate he might have been excused. But to do a thing like that at forty . . . For a woman. Well . . .

20 *A pilgrim*
To be
a pilgrim
is
to be
at home
in the world
at large.
It is
to be
at home
and
on one's way
home
at the same time.

21 *Perfect*
You are
perfect.
He is
imperfect.
I am
past perfect.
Do you still
care for
me
darling?
Am I still

present
in your thoughts
at dawn?

22 *Man and wife*
We are dreaming
two separate dreams
about the world.
We are living
in two different worlds
side by side.
We are walking
across life
hand in hand,
a loving husband
and a loving wife
worlds apart.

23 *To emigrate?*
You've left
it all
behind.
All unnecessary things:
the landscapes
of the past,
the language
and

the low living standards.
Facing
new challenges,
you have
no time
to think
or to remember.
At long last
you've become
part of
what you'll never be able
to understand.

24   *A chance to win*
Oh God,
why did you
dream me
in such a way
that I can't
resist the temptation
to question things?
Did you need
a partner
for a game
of chess?
Are you
prepared
to give me
a chance
to win?

25   *My father*
Tomorrow
I'll be
twice as old
as you were
when you died.
Our roles
seem
to have changed.
Don't you think
it's time

I stopped thinking of you
as my father?
That phase is past.
What matters
lies ahead.

26   *What is meaning?*
It is
the space
around a star.
It is
the time
before and after
being together.
It is
the silence
between one word and
    another.
It is
what is
around
what is not.

27   *Until last night*
She died
at the age
of eighty-four
fourteen years ago.
I never gave her
much thought
afterwards.
Until last night
when she came
in a dream;
a beautiful young girl
I had never seen before.
But I knew
it was her.
Must have been
her smile
that I recognized
at once.

Epitaphs are short texts written to commemorate someone's death. They are usually carved on a gravestone or on a memorial plaque. Sometimes people write their own epitaphs before they die. In other cases they are written by others after their death. Although death is a serious matter, it is not unusual for epitaphs to express a macabre kind of humour.

The Sample Text:
Grim Death took me without any warning,
I was well at night –
And dead at nine in the morning.
Gravestone at Sevenoaks, Kent

1 EXPANSION

a) Add further information to the text by giving details about what happened the previous day.
   e.g. I was well at night – I'd had a tiring day, so I decided to relax in the evening. Some friends came for dinner, then we watched TV for a bit . . .
b) Add a final line (or lines) to the epitaph as a kind of commentary. (These need not ryhme.)
   e.g. • I hardly think it's fair
        • To be taken unaware.
        • He might have let me know
        • That it was time for me to go.

2 REDUCTION

Shorten the epitaph by reducing it to six essential words only.
e.g. Without warning:
     Night – well,
     Morning – dead.

3 MEDIA TRANSFER

a) Write a brief obituary notice as it might appear in the classified ads section of a newspaper. You will need to invent the name and age of the person who died.

e.g. Joseph Newnham passed away suddenly at 9 a.m. on Tuesday, 6th May aged 40. Deeply mourned by wife Margaret and daughter Sarah. Funeral St Marks, Bell Lane at 10.00 on 12th May. No flowers.

b) Write a brief stop-press news item for a newspaper based on the epitaph.

e.g. *Grim Reaper strikes at his home*
Local businessman Joseph Newnham died at his home following a stroke at 09.00 on Tuesday, 6th May. He was 40. He had never experienced a day's illness previously and had dined out with business associates the evening before. As a councillor he was well known to all in the local community and will be greatly missed. He leaves his wife Margaret and a daughter, Sarah. (Ed.)

4 MATCHING

a) Which of the obituaries matches best with the original?

i)   To our son Benjamin Baker
Who returned to his Maker
After a long illness, patiently borne.
He left us 10 years old – is now re-born.

ii) *To Harry Franks*
He lived his life fast;
Knew it could not last.
One day he was there,
The next gone. (where?)

iii) Margaret Mason lies under this stone.
In life she was a light in my darkness,
Till a thunderbolt snuffed her out,
Leaving me in shadow and alone.
George Mason, Husband

b) Check the other epitaphs in this section and see if you can find one which matches closely in meaning with the original.

5 SELECTION/RANKING

a) See the epitaphs in 4a) above. Place these in order from most to least like the original.

b) Look at the other epitaphs in this section. With a partner decide which is:
• the funniest
• the saddest
• the cruellest

- the most cynical
- the most moving

6 COMPARISON/CONTRAST

Here is a comic poem:

'I've never felt finer,'
Said the King of China,
Sitting down to dine.
Then he fell down dead.
He died, he did.
It was only half-past nine.
> *Spike Milligan*

Compare this with the epitaph. What things does it contain which are the same as in the epitaph? Are there any differences? Why isn't it an epitaph?

7 RECONSTRUCTION

In this epitaph, the words in each line are jumbled. Put them into the correct order:

- any without took warning Grim me Death
- at well I night was
- at dead morning in and nine The

8 REFORMULATION

a) Read the epitaph again. Then put it away. Write out the message of the epitaph in your own words from memory.

b) Here are some keywords from the epitaph you have read. Without looking at the original, rewrite the epitaph in your own words using the keywords to help you.

Death without warning dead well night nine morning

9 INTERPRETATION

a) What questions might you want to put to the author? (e.g. Who? How? Where? etc.)

b) When was the epitaph written – before or after the death? Who could *not* have written it?

c) What information does the epitaph leave out?

d) Does this incident remind you of any experience you yourself have had?

10 CREATING TEXT

a) Write a second 'verse' to the epitaph which explains the cause of death.

e.g. As I sat down to break my fast
I felt a sudden pain.
I knew these breaths would be my last,
That I'd not break fast again.

b) Write a haiku which uses the same information as the epitaph.

e.g. I was well at night,
but Grim Death took me at dawn
light became darkness

11 ANALYSIS

a) We often talk indirectly about dying. For example, instead of saying someone died, we say they 'passed away' or 'left us' or 'went to his Maker' etc. We call this a euphemism. There is a euphemism in this epitaph. Can you find it?

b) Notice that the epitaph is constructed in a way which is quite common in English. In line 1 we have a statement of what happened, followed by lines 2 and 3 which expand the information given in the first line.

Look through the other epitaphs in this section to see if you can find any which use this construction.

12 PROJECT WORK

a) In groups, check on the obituary columns of some English-language newspapers. Make a collection of the obituaries of some of the more interesting people and prepare a classroom display.

b) If you are in an English-speaking country, arrange to visit a local churchyard or cemetery. In groups, make a collection of any especially interesting items you find and prepare a display based upon them.

Some further ideas

In order to familiarize students with the range of texts in this section it is a good idea to set some global tasks to begin with. For example:

a) Group together all those epitaphs which are:
  • about a violent death.
    e.g. 'John Bunn'
  • are cynical/sarcastic
    e.g. 'Owen Moore'
  • genuinely grief-stricken
    e.g. 'To our adopted son Norman'

b) Are there other ways you could group the epitaphs?

Activities which work well with epitaphs include:
3 Media transfer, 4 Matching, 8 Reformulation, 9 Interpretation,
12 Project work.

Epitaphs

1 Here lies John Bunn,
   Who was killed by a gun,
   His name wasn't Bunn, his real
      name was Wood,
   But Wood wouldn't rhyme with gun, so
      I thought Bunn should.
            From a gravestone in Southampton, Hampshire

2 Blown Upward
      Out of Sight
   He Sought The Leak
      By Candlelight
            On a headstone in Collingbourne Ducis, Wiltshire

3 *Owen Moore*
   Gone away
   Ow'n more
   Than he could pay.
            In St John's Church, Battersea, London

4 God works wonders now and then;
   Here lies a lawyer and an honest man.

   To which an unknown hand has added:

   This is a mere law quibble, not a
      wonder:
   Here lies a lawyer, and his client under.
            From a memorial stone in Walworth, London

5 Remember me as you pass by
   As you are now, so once was I,
   As I am now, you soon will be,
   Therefore prepare to follow me.

To which was later added:

> To follow you I'm not content
> Until I know which way you went.
>> *On a grave in Great Burstead Church, Essex*

6 Life is a jest, and all things show it;
  I thought so once, now I know it.
>> *On tomb of the poet John Gay in Westminster Abbey*

7 Here lies one who for medicines would
      not give
  A little gold, and so his life he lost;
  I fancy now he'd wish again to live,
  Could he but guess how much his
      funeral cost.
>> *In Sheffield cemetery, Yorkshire*

8 Underneath his ancient mill
  Lies the body of poor Will;
  Odd he lived and odd he died,
  And at his funeral nobody cried;
  Where he's gone and how he fares,
  Nobody knows, and nobody cares.
>> *In Canterbury cemetery, Kent*

9 If there is a future world
      My lot will not be bliss;
  But if there is no other
      I've made the most of this.
>> *From Desingwoke cemetery, USA*

10 Here lies my poor wife,
       A sad slatern and shrew,
   If I said I regretted her
       I should lie too.
>> *On a headstone in Texas, USA*

11 He died in peace
       His wife died first.
>> *On a grave in Ilfracombe cemetery, Devon*

12 Here lies my adviser, Dr. Sim,
     And those he healed – near him.
          In Grimsby Parish Church, Humberside

13 Some have children, some have none;
     Here lies the mother of 21.
          On the headstone of Ann Jennings, in Wolstanston cemetery,
          Cheshire

14 *Jemmy Wyatt*
     At rest beneath this churchyard stone,
     Lies stingy Jemmy Wyatt;
     He died one morning just at ten,
     And saved a dinner by it!
          On a disappeared grave in Studley churchyard, Wiltshire

15 *Peter Robinson*
     Here lies the preacher, judge
          And poet, Peter:
     Who broke the laws of
          God and Man
          And meter.
          On a headstone in Bristol cemetery, Avon

16 *On the setting up of Mr Butler's monument in*
     Westminster Abbey
     While Butler, needy wretch, was yet alive,
     No generous patron would a dinner give;
     See him, when starved to death and turned to dust,
     Presented with a monumental bust!
     The poet's fate is here in emblem shown:
     He asked for bread, and he received a stone.

17 To our adopted son Norman,
     Who died of diabetes, aged three.
     The priest told us in the sermon
     It was God's will – let's see!

18 In this grave lies Michael Partridge,
     Whose body's now an empty cartridge.
     He thought the safety-catch was on
     It wasn't – that is why he's gone.

19 Dear passerby remember Catherine Stone,
   Who choked to death on a herring bone.
   Those present heard her, as she died, say
   'Thanks be to God it was a Friday!'

20 Here lie the bones of Mary Lunn,
   Who died in bringing forth a son.
   That son now offers up his prayers,
   Hoping Mother Lunn has gone *up*stairs.

21 In this dark grave lies Miss Jane Key,
   Whose life was ended by a bee.
   While she was out collecting honey,
   It stung her on the lip – not funny!

22 The poor remains of Peter Pound
   Are slowly rotting underground.
   It's sad but true to have to say
   That you and I will end that way.

23 In life John Simpson was a beast.
   Now worms and maggots have a feast.
   There now remains a final question –
   Will they succumb to indigestion?

24 Though Peter Prout was a Boy Scout,
   He could not find his way about.
   Aged 15 years he lost his way –
   Now he's beneath 6 feet of clay.

25 Two yards under this cold stone
   There was once flesh – now only bone.
   Now that his eyes are only sockets,
   My husband's cash is in my pockets.

26 Here lie the remains of William Pitt,
   In life renowned as wag and wit.
   Now that his mouth is stopped with clay,
   There's nothing left for him to say.

27 Time they say will take its toll
And send us upward to our God.
But really it's the worm and mole
That toil beneath the graveyard sod.

Diaries are endlessly fascinating for the glimpses they give of the writer's intimate character. The diaries of Samuel Pepys, John Evelyn and the Rev. Francis Kilvert are deservedly famous. But many equally famous, as well as completely unknown, people have kept diaries for longer or shorter periods of their lives.

The Sample Text:
13th February 1956
In the hope of understanding Bron better I read the diaries I kept at his age. I was appalled at the vulgarity and priggishness.
Evelyn Waugh

1 EXPANSION
Expand the text by adding as many adjectives and adverbs as you can.
e.g. In the *vain* hope of understanding Bron *slightly* better I *carefully* read the *youthful* diaries I had *foolishly* kept at his *tender* age . . .

2 REDUCTION
Shorten the entry very slightly by changing the structure of the two sentences.
e.g. Hoping to . . . The vulgarity and priggishness were . . .

3 MEDIA TRANSFER
a) Use the information from the diary entry to write a short letter to a friend.
e.g. Dear Tom,
As you know I've been worried about Bron recently. I thought it might be helpful if I . . .
b) Write out the message of the text as a haiku.
e.g. • reading the diary
I'd written when I was young –
oh the priggishness!
• to understand him

> I read my childhood diaries –
> how ashamed I felt!

c) Write a piece of dialogue from a radio play based on the life of Evelyn Waugh.

> e.g. X. How are things between you and Bron these days?
> E. W. Funny you should ask. As a matter of fact, I thought it might help if I . . .

4 MATCHING

a) Match the text with the paraphrase which corresponds most closely to its meaning.

   i)   When the writer read his son's diary he was appalled.
   ii) When the writer read his own youthful diaries he was shocked.
   iii) When the writer read Bron's youthful diaries he found them vulgar.

b) Look at the section on one-liners (pp. 15–16). Try to find a proverb which roughly matches this text.

5 SELECTION/RANKING

a) Put these titles for the passage in order from most to least suitable:
   • Never Look Back
   • Understanding Who?
   • The Damning Diary
   • Like Son, Like Father

b) Here are three diary entries about the same incident in three different styles. Put them in order from most to least formal.

   i)   In the hope of understanding Bron better I read the diaries I kept at his age. I was appalled at the vulgarity and priggishness.
   ii) I thought I might stand a better chance of understanding Bron if I checked back on what I was like at his age, so I've read some of my own teenage diaries. My God! What a shock! I'd never realized how stuck up and vulgar I was.
   iii) It occurred to me in a moment of inspiration that I might acquire a better insight into Bron's behaviour were I to reread the journals I had myself kept at his age. I found myself appalled at the sheer vulgarity and priggishness which they revealed.

6 COMPARISON/CONTRAST

Read the following poem. List all the similarities and differences you can find between it and the diary entry.

Growing Up?

It must be, oooh,
a month or more
since they last complained
about the way I eat
or crisps I drop
on the kitchen floor
or not washing my feet
or the TV left on
when I go out
or the spoon clunking
against my teeth
or how loudly I shout
or my unmade bed,
mud on the stair,
soap left to drown
or the state of my hair . . .
It *must* be
a month or more.
Have they given up
in despair?
For years
they've nagged me
to grow up,
to act my age.
Can it be
that it's happened,
that I'm ready
to step out of my cage?
    Wes Magee

7 RECONSTRUCTION
This diary entry has a number of gaps in it. Try to write in the
words you think fit best:

    In the _____ of understanding Bron _____ I _____
    the diaries I kept at his _____. I was _____ at the
    vulgarity and _____.

8 REFORMULATION
a) Rewrite the diary extract in an optimistic, positive tone. You only
need to change *three* words.

b) Here are outline notes for a diary entry. Use them to write the entry.
- Problems with Bron.
- Reread own diaries (schooldays) – possible help?
- Shock! Very vulgar/priggish.

9 INTERPRETATION

a) Does this diary entry 'ring true'? Can you remember anything about your own earlier life which might embarrass you now? Did you keep a diary then?

b) What do you think the relationship is between the writer and Bron?

c) Do you keep a diary (or have you ever kept one)? What did you find the most difficult problem? (Keeping it up regularly? Being honest with yourself? Knowing how much to write? etc.)

10 CREATING TEXT

Write a brief diary extract about one incident which has happened to you within the past week.

11 ANALYSIS

There is no obvious, explicit link between the two sentences of the text. The reader is expected to make the connection for himself. Try to rewrite the text supplying an explicit link.

e.g. . . . at his age. *When I did* I was appalled . . .

. . . at his age. *They came as a complete surprise to me.* I was appalled . . .

. . . at his age. *The result of this was not what I had expected.* I was appalled . . .

12 PROJECT WORK

a) Start a class diary. Each day a different person (or group) takes the responsibility for writing an entry. The entries can be displayed on the class notice-board.

b) If class members are willing, it may be of interest for those who have kept diaries in the past to bring them in and to read out certain parts of them.

Those who did not keep diaries may interview those who did to find out their attitudes to the 'former self' which the diaries reveal. It will be necessary to draw up a questionnaire in advance of the interviews.

Some further ideas

It will help if students form an overall idea of the kind of diary entries in this section before concentrating on particular texts.

Here are some possible activities:

a) Which of the diarists would you most have liked to meet? Which least?

b) Can you tell how old the writers were when they wrote these entries?

c) Which is the saddest entry?

Which the happiest?

Which the funniest?

In general, the activities which work best with diary entries are:

1 Expansion, 2 Reduction, 3 Media transfer, 5 Selection/ranking, 6 Comparison/contrast, 8 Reformulation, 9 Interpretation, 12 Project work.

Diary entries

1 1875 When I went to bed last night I fancied that something ran in at my bedroom door after me from the gallery. It seemed to be a skeleton. It ran with a dancing step and I thought it aimed a blow at me from behind. This was shortly before midnight.

The Reverend Francis Kilvert

2 1927 Beginning to feel that I ought not to be long with the BBC, but it is extremely difficult to find what the next job is to be. So few good jobs or ones that I would like at all. What a curse it is to have outstanding comprehensive ability and intelligence, combined with a desire to use them to maximum purpose.

John Reith

3 1661 At the office all the morning. Dined at home. And after dinner to Mr Crews and thence to the Theatre, where I saw again *The Lost Lady*, which doth now please me better then before. And here, I sitting behind in a dark place, a lady spat backward upon me by a mistake, not seeing me. But after seeing her to be a very pretty lady, I was not troubled at it at all.

Samuel Pepys

4 1935 Came back after dinner to meet Winston Churchill, who was very pleasant and seemed to appreciate my staying to meet him. His talk on India was awfully disappointing – a string of bombastic phrases with little sincerity at the back of it. Finished up by borrowing 5/- from me.
John Reith

5 1828 I am, I find, in serious danger of losing the habit of my journal and having carried it on so long that would be pity. But I am now on the 1st february fishing for the lost recollections of the days since the 21 January. Luckily there is not very much to remember or forget and perhaps the best way would be to skip and go on.
Sir Walter Scott

6 1934 My 35th birthday. Actually I have lied so much about my age that I forget how old I really am. I think I look 28, and know I feel 19.
'Chips' Channon

7 1946 I had a poem in my head last night, flashing as only those unformed midnight poems can. It was all made up of unexpected burning words. I knew even in my half-sleep that it was nonsense, meaningless, but that forcing and hammering would clear its shape and form. Now not a word of it remains, not even a hint of its direction. What a pity one cannot sleepwrite on the ceiling with one's finger or lifted toe.
Denton Welch

8 1980 Children and grandchildren arrive. Cold wind, hot sun, blue sea. Read Ruskin, walk on the beach, play snakes and ladders. Feel well blessed. What did Thomas More say to his children? 'I have given you, forsooth, kisses in plenty and but few stripes . . . If ever I have flogged you 'twas but with a peacock's tail.'
Hugh Casson

9 1875 We took tea with Mr Hipperson of Hoe. The whole thing was done rather as a joke, and the old lady provided hot cockles, which our party had never tasted before, and which we are in no hurry to taste again.
The Reverend Benjamin Armstrong

10 1936   Kit is in hospital. I went to see her this afternoon. After I'd
left the hospital, I walked along the Embankment worrying
about her, imagining how I'd react if she died, then realiz-
ing that I was turning even the possibility of her death into
a kind of sensuality.
Malcolm Muggeridge

11 1911   London. Palace Theatre. Pavlova dancing the dying swan.
Feather falls off her dress. Two silent Englishmen. One
says, 'Moulting'. That is all they say.
Arnold Bennett

12 1948   I quite often look back at the pleasures and pains of youth
– love, jealousy, recklessness, vanity – without forgetting
their spell but no longer desiring them; while middle-aged
ones like music, places, botany, conversation seem to be
just as enjoyable as those wilder ones, in which there was
usually some potential anguish lying in wait, like a bee in
a flower. I hope there may be further surprises in store,
and on the whole do not fear the advance into age.
Frances Partridge

13 1941   This is the eighth day of my renunciation of smoking. It
gets more difficult rather than less difficult. But I do
observe that it is a thought which suggests a pang rather
than a pang which suggests a thought. Thus an aching
tooth twitches into consciousness and says 'I have a tooth-
ache.' But this nicotine hunger is only stimulated by some
outside occurrence such as the sight of someone else smoking or an advertisement of Craven A. Then the pang lights
up. Apart from that it is a vague feeling of something
missing as if one had had no breakfast.
???

14 1831   I wonder if I shall burn this sheet of paper like most others
I have begun in the same way. To write a diary, I have
thought of how very often at far & near distance of time:
but how could I write a diary without throwing upon
paper my thoughts, all my thoughts – the thoughts of my
heart as well as of my head? – & then how could I bear to
look on *them* after they were written? Adam made fig
leaves necessary for the mind, as well as for the body. And

such *a* mind as I have! – So very exacting & exclusive &
eager & head long – & *strong* – & so very often *wrong*! Well!
but I will write: I must write – & the oftener wrong I
know myself to be, the less wrong I shall be in one thing
– the less *vain* I shall be! –

Elizabeth Barrett

15 1939 On the hottest day of the year I saw two nuns buying a
typewriter in Selfridges. Oh, what were they going to do
with it?

Barbara Pym

16 1914 There has been another assassination, this time of the heir
of the Austrian Emperor. I do not quite know how it
affects the political situation.

Wilfred Scawen Blunt

17 1946 Well, the atom bomb experiment was made last night,
with apparently disappointing results. I would like it put
on record that I think now, and always have thought, that
far too much cock has been talked about atomic energy. I
have no more faith in men of science being infallible than
I have in men of God being infallible, principally on
account of them being men. I have heard it stated that
atomic energy might disturb the course of the earth
through the universe; that it might cause devastating tidal
waves; that it might transform climates from hot to cold
or vice versa; make a hole in the bed of the ocean so that
the seas would drain away and extinguish the fires of the
earth; suddenly deflect out planet into the orbit of the sun,
in which case we should all shrivel up, etc., etc., etc. I am
convinced that all it will really do is destroy human beings
in large numbers. I have a feeling that the universe and the
laws of nature are beyond its scope.

Noël Coward

18 1955 I am amazed that life seems to get more and more interesting as one gets older – and also perhaps saner, serener,
more tough. It is no doubt the Indian Summer before the
hand of decrepitude strikes and health crumbles.

Frances Partridge

19 1763 I remember nothing that happened worth relating this day.
How many such days does mortal man pass!
James Boswell

20 1945 The world has been electrified, thrilled and horrified by
the atomic bomb; one has been dropped in Japan today. It
devastated a whole town and killed a quarter of a million
people. It could mean the end of civilization.
'Chips' Channon

21 1864 The day was devoted to looking over old letters – a necessary task, and the sense of its being a duty almost its only
inducement. Some of the old letters were sour-sweet; but
it was more painful than pleasant ruminating on them.
Henry Crabb Robinson

22 1980 All day drawing. On the way to a quick office lunch pass
a nun changing a wheel in Cromwell Road. Ashamed to
say I don't stop to help.
Hugh Casson

23 1872 Maria told us the story of Anna Kilvert and the cat, and
the Epiphany Star. It seems that when Aunt Sophia was
dying Anna thought some mutton would do her good and
went to fetch some. When she came back the nurse said,
'She can't eat mutton. She's dying.' Anna put the mutton
down on the floor and rushed to the bed. At that moment
Aunt Sophia died and Anna turned round to see the cat
running away with the mutton and the Epiphany Star
shining in through the window.
The Reverend Francis Kilvert

24 1981 Stepping across the gate into Sarah's arms. We embrace
and kiss. So lovely to touch in legitimate time. We waste
no time jumping in the car and heading into the distance.
  Accumulated thoughts: I am wondering what it will be
like to sleep together, having known each other for four
years and been married almost two. Up the long winding
roads the scenery was spectacular. Sitting there with Sarah
at my side, the prison far behind and the wonders of the
Scottish Highlands all around me I felt stunned with
pleasure . . . How can I possibly explain this experience to

anyone after fourteen years in prison? Every fibre was open and alert to this vast mountain scenery. Finally we reached our caravan situated high up on the hillside with a wide and full view of the valley. It was getting quite dark though still enough light for us to see our view from the caravan. Sheep were all around us. We looked down the valley to a spattering of cottages and farmhouses. The visual images were overwhelming. The night was spent in a small double bed with me always aware of Sarah next to me. I was restless. It will take some getting used to after fourteen years of sleeping alone . . . It's the first time in years I've slept on a mattress.

Jimmy Boyle

25 1949 Tomorrow is my father's birthday. He would have been seventy-seven. I never think of him.

'Chips' Channon

26 1813 Went to bed, and slept dreamlessly, but not refreshingly. Awoke, and up an hour before being called; but dawdled three hours in dressing. When one subtracts from life infancy (which is vegetation) – sleep, eating, and swilling – buttoning and unbuttoning – how much remains of downright existence? The summer of a dormouse.

Lord Byron

27 1915 Sunday December 26th
Directly after breakfast I went down to Brighton, sent on my way with many good wishes from the others. I walked along the promenade, and looked at the grey sea tossing rough with white surf-crested waves, and felt a little anxiety at the kind of crossing he had had. But at any rate he should be safely in England by this time, though he probably has not been able to send me any message to-day owing to the difficulties of telephones and telegrams on Sunday & Christmas Day combined, & the inaccessibility of Hassocks. So I only have to wait for the morrow with such patience as I can manage. Being a little tired with the energies of the night, I spent a good deal of the rest of the day in sleeping, thinking of the sweet anticipation of the morning and of the face and voice dearest of all to me on earth.

Vera Brittain

28 1915 Monday December 27th
         I had just finished dressing when a message came to say
         that there was a telephone message for me. I sprang up
         joyfully, thinking to hear in a moment the dear dreamed-
         of tones of the beloved voice.
             But the telephone message was not from Roland but
         from Clare; it was not to say that Roland had arrived, but
         that instead had come this telegram, sent on to the Leigh-
         tons by Mr Burgin, to whom for some time all corres-
         pondence sent to Lowestoft had been readdressed:
         T 233. Regret to inform you that Lieut. R. A. Leighton
         7th Worcesters died of wounds December 23rd. Lord
         Kitchener sends his sympathy.
             Colonel of Territorial Force, Records, Warwick.
             Vera Brittain

29 1914 The year is nearly over. Snow has fallen, and everything
         is white. It is very cold. I have changed the position of my
         desk into a corner. Perhaps I shall be able to write far more
         easily here. Yes, this is a good place for the desk, because
         I cannot see out of the stupid window. I am quite private.
         The lamp stands on one corner and *in* the corner. Its rays
         fall on the yellow and green Indian curtain and on the strip
         of red embroidery. The forlorn wind scarcely breathes. I
         love to close my eyes a moment and think of the land
         outside, white under the mingled snow and moonlight –
         white trees, white fields – the heaps of stones by the road-
         side white – snow in the furrows. *Mon Dieu*! How quiet
         and how patient! If he were to come I could not even hear
         his footsteps.
             Katherine Mansfield

30 1915 *New Year's Eve 11.55 2 The Crescent, Keymer, Hassocks,*
         Sussex
         This time last year He was seeing me off on Charing Cross
         Station after *David Copperfield* – and I had just begun to
         realise I loved Him. To-day He is lying in the military
         cemetery at Louvencourt – because a week ago He was
         wounded in action, and had just 24 hours of consciousness
         more and then went "to sleep in France". And I, who in
         impatience felt a fortnight ago that I could not wait another
         minute to see Him, must wait till all Eternity. All has been

given me, and all taken away again – in one year.

So I wonder where we shall be – what we shall all be doing – if we all still *shall* be – this time next year.

Vera Brittain

Poems are not necessarily 'more difficult' than prose, as many people think, but they *are* different. One thing that makes them different is that they are often written within stricter 'rules' than prose (rhyme, rhythm, metre etc.). They also tend to squeeze more meaning out of fewer words. So they are both more complex and more condensed than 'ordinary' language. But this means that they are also more interesting.

The Sample Text:

The Miniature

The grey beards wag, the bald heads nod,
And gather thick as bees,
To talk electrons, gases, God,
Old nebulae, new fleas.
Each specialist, each dry-as-dust
And professorial oaf,
Holds up his little crumb of crust
And cries, 'Behold the loaf!'

    Eden Phillpotts

I EXPANSION
a) Write a short paragraph (in prose) which could precede the poem and another one which could follow it, as a kind of conclusion.
b) Try writing a new verse before and after the poem.

e.g. *before*: The conference of experts has begun,
        Uniting the great brains of the world.
        Each speciality's represented, every one
        As the banner of science is unfurled.

  after: How futile their puny understanding seems.
        However grandiose the claims they make,
        If no one can agree to share their schemes,
        Surely it's one colossal, daft mistake.

c) Some insertion markers ($\mathcal{L}$) have been put in this version of the poem. Put the words from the list below into the places you feel they fit best.

The *ʎ* grey beards wag, the *ʎ* bald heads nod,
And gather thick as *ʎ* bees,
To talk electrons, *ʎ* gases, God,
Old *ʎ* nebulae, new fleas.
Each *ʎ* specialist, each dry-as-dust
And professional *ʎ* oaf,
Holds up his *ʎ* little crumb of crust
And cries, 'Behold the *ʎ* loaf!'
buzzing blindfold sounding universal protons long dried-up style old
Does the poem still 'sound right'?

2 REDUCTION

Remove as many articles, joining words and adjectives as you can, so as to shorten the poem.
e.g. Beards wag, heads nod,
Gather thick as bees,
Talk electrons, gases, God,
Nebulae and fleas.
Each specialist, dry-as-dust,
Professorial oaf
Holds up his crumb of crust,
Cries, 'Behold the loaf!'

3 MEDIA TRANSFER

Write out the message of the poem as a letter to a friend.
e.g. Dear Peter,
I went to one of those big scientific conferences last week.
All sorts of specialists were there . . .
Compare your version with your partner's.

4 MATCHING

a) Match the poem with one of these alternative titles:
Whose Truth?
Intellectual Arrogance
Food for Thought
Bread and Circuses
b) Check the sections on one-liners (p. 11), Nasruddin stories (p. 107) and short essays (p. 118). See if you can match the poem with any of the items in these three sections.

5 SELECTION/RANKING

Decide on an order from most suitable to least suitable for the purposes to which the poem might be put.

a) as a quotation in a speech by the Minister for Science and Technology to The Royal Society (the most famous scientific academy in Britain)

b) as the first paragraph of an article in a religious magazine

c) as part of an advertisement for bread

d) as a poem for inclusion in an anthology for young children

6 COMPARISON/CONTRAST

a)   Compare the original with this poem:

The Purist

I give you now Professor Twist,
A conscientious scientist.
Trustees exclaimed, 'He never bungles!'
And sent him off to distant jungles.
Camped on a tropic riverside,
One day he missed his loving bride.
She had, the guide informed him later,
Been eaten by an alligator.
Professor Twist could not but smile.
'You mean,' he said, 'a crocodile.'
        Ogden Nash

Are there any ideas which are common to the two poems? Are there any other things which they both have? (e.g. rhyme, length, same words etc.)

b) Compare the poem with the story of the blind men and the elephant. What is similar? What is different?

The Blind Men and the Elephant

It was six men of Hindostan,
To learning much inclined,
Who went to see the elephant
(Though all of them were blind);
That each by observation
Might satisfy his mind.

The first approached the elephant,
And happening to fall
Against his broad and sturdy side,
At once began to bawl,
'Bless me, it seems the elephant
Is very like a wall.'

The second, feeling of his tusk,
Cried, 'Ho! what have we here
So very round and smooth and sharp?
To me 'tis mighty clear
This wonder of an elephant
Is very like a spear.'

The third approached the animal,
And happening to take
The squirming trunk within his hands,
Then boldly up and spake;
'I see,' quoth he, 'the elephant
Is very like a snake.'

The fourth stretched out his eager hand
And felt about the knee,
'What most this mighty beast is like
Is mighty plain,' quoth he;
''Tis clear enough the elephant
Is very like a tree.'

The fifth who chanced to touch the ear
Said, 'Even the blindest man
Can tell what this resembles most;
Deny the fact who can,
This marvel of an elephant
Is very like a fan.'

The sixth no sooner had begun
About the beast to grope
Than, seizing on the swinging tail
That fell within his scope,
'I see,' cried he, 'the elephant
Is very like a rope.'

And so these men of Hindostan
Disputed loud and long,
Each of his own opinion

Exceeding stiff and strong,
Though each was partly in the right,
And all were in the wrong.
    John Godfrey Saxe

7 RECONSTRUCTION

a) The lines of this poem are in the wrong order. Try to rearrange
them in an order which makes sense for you:

The Miniature

Each specialist, each dry-as-dust
And cries, 'Behold the loaf!'
The grey beards wag, the bald heads nod,
And professorial oaf,
Old nebulae, new fleas.
To talk electrons, gases, God,
Holds up his little crumb of crust
And gather thick as bees,

b) Remove words from this version of the poem which do not seem
to fit properly.

The Miniature

The grey beards wag, the bald red heads nod,
And gather thick as queen bees,
To talk about electrons, poisonous gases, God almighty,
Old tired nebulae, new born fleas.
Each rich specialist, each famous dry-as-dust
And well-known professorial oaf,
Holds up aloft his little mouldy crumb of crust
And cries aloud, 'Behold the universal loaf!'

Remember that this is a poem which should rhyme and have a
regular rhythm.

8 REFORMULATION

Read the poem for 5–10 minutes. Then put it away and rewrite
it from memory. When you have written as much as possible,
work with a partner comparing your versions.

9 INTERPRETATION

a) What pictures (images) does the poem spark off in your mind? What memories of real occasions have you experienced yourself?

b) Who do you think is speaking in the poem?

c) Why do you think it has the title 'The Miniature'? Can you think of a better title?

d) Write out in prose what you think is the message which the poem is trying to convey.

  e.g. Every expert thinks he knows the whole truth whereas he only really knows a tiny part of it.

  Is this true as far as *your* experience goes?

e) How would you describe the *tone* of the poem?

  respectful?, ironic?, comic?, sarcastic?, cynical?, admiring?, indifferent?, angry?, despairing? . . .

10 CREATING TEXT

a) Write a haiku (see p. 18) or a tanka (see p. 21) with the same message as the poem.

  e.g. when I got too close
        to the words on the paper –
        I couldn't read them!

b) If you can, write a verse which could fit into the middle of the poem.

  e.g. (Old nebulae, new fleas).
        The ideas fly, the battles rage
        And reputations tumble.
        The experts strut upon the stage
        And only rarely stumble.
        (Each specialist . . .)

11 ANALYSIS

a) Which is the tense used throughout the poem? Is there a reason for this? (Why isn't it in the past tense?)

b) Look for the rhyme scheme of the poem. Is it regular?

c) Look for alliteration in the poem. (Alliteration is when several neighbouring words begin with the same sound, e.g. dry-as-dust.)

d) Are there any examples of assonance in the poem? (Assonance is when several neighbouring vowel sounds are the same, e.g. crumb of crust.)

e) Make a list of the things we know from the poem because they are *stated* and those that we can *infer*.

e.g. We can infer that the poet is talking about a specific scientific conference *or* about scientists in general.

12 PROJECT WORK

Work in a group to devise a questionnaire which asks some fundamental questions (e.g. What is truth? What is reality? What is air? What does morality mean? What is learning? etc.)

Then interview as many people as you can from different specialist backgrounds. (banking, business, computer technology, science etc.)

Compare and tabulate the answers to the questions and prepare a visual display for the notice-board.

Some further ideas

Try to set up some activities which will ensure that the students have to have looked at all the texts in the unit, before homing in on specific texts. For example:

a) Which of the poems deal with concrete, specific experiences? (e.g. 'The Eagle', 'Maternity', 'D is for Dog' etc.)

b) Which ones deal with observations about life in general? (e.g. 'Plays', 'Below the surface-stream', 'The Adversary' etc.)

c) How many of them are about animals and how many about people?

d) How many of them rhyme?

e) Which one would you prefer to hear being read aloud?

The activities which tend to work best with short poems are:

1 Expansion, 2 Reduction, 3 Media transfer, 4 Matching, 6 Comparison/contrast, 7 Reconstruction, 9 Interpretation, 10 Creating text, 11 Analysis.

Short poems

1 *Plays*

Alas, how soon the hours are over,
Counted us out to play the lover!
And how much narrower is the stage,
Allotted us to play the sage!

But when we play the fool, how wide
The theatre expands! beside,

How long the audience sits before us!
How many prompters! what a chorus!
    Walter Savage Landor

2 The Eagle

He clasps the crag with crooked hands;
Close to the sun in lonely lands,
Ringed with the azure world, he stands.

The wrinkled sea beneath him crawls;
He watches from his mountain walls,
And like a thunderbolt he falls.
    Alfred, Lord Tennyson

3 'Below the surface-stream'

Below the surface-stream, shallow and light,
Of what we *say* we feel – below the stream,
As light, of what we *think* we feel – there flows
With noiseless current strong, obscure and deep,
The central stream of what we feel indeed.
    Matthew Arnold

4 'To spend uncounted years of pain'

To spend uncounted years of pain,
Again, again, and yet again,
In working out in heart and brain
    The problem of our being here;
To gather facts from far and near,
Upon the mind to hold them clear,
And, knowing more may yet appear,
Unto one's latest breath to fear
The premature result to draw –
Is this the object, end, and law,
    And purpose of our being here?
    Arthur Hugh Clough

5 Maternity

One wept whose only child was dead,
New-born, ten years ago.
'Weep not; he is in bliss,' they said.
She answered, 'Even so,

'Ten years ago was born in pain
A child, not now forlorn.
But oh, ten years ago, in vain,
A mother, a mother was born.'
  Alice Meynell

6 *The Night Has a Thousand Eyes*

The night has a thousand eyes,
 And the day but one;
Yet the light of the bright world dies
 With the dying sun.

The mind has a thousand eyes,
 And the heart but one;
Yet the light of a whole life dies
 When love is gone.
  Francis William Bourdillon

7 *D is for Dog*

My dog went mad and bit my hand,
 I was bitten to the bone:
My wife went walking out with him,
 And then came back alone.

I smoked my pipe, I nursed my wound,
 I saw them both depart:
And when my wife came back alone,
 I was bitten to the heart.
  W.H. Davies

8 *Dust of Snow*

The way a crow
Shook down on me
The dust of snow
From a hemlock tree

Has given my heart
A change of mood
And saved some part
Of a day I had rued.
  Robert Frost

9 *The Adversary*

> A mother's hardest to forgive.
> Life is the fruit she longs to hand you,
> Ripe on a plate. And while you live,
> Relentlessly she understands you.
> > *Phyllis McGinley*

10 *The Lovers*

> After the tiff there was stiff silence, till
> One word, flung in centre like single stone,
> Starred and cracked the ice of her resentment
> To its edge. From that stung core opened and
> Poured up one outward and widening wave
> Of eager and extravagant anger.
> > *W.R. Rodgers*

11 *Triolet*

> When first we met we did not guess
> That Love would prove so hard a master;
> Of more than common friendliness
> When first we met we did not guess.
> Who could foretell this sore distress,
> This irretrievable disaster
> When first we met? – We did not guess
> That Love would prove so hard a master.
> > *Robert Bridges*

12 *Ending*

> The love we thought would never stop
> now cools like a congealing chop.
> The kisses that were hot as curry
> are bird-pecks taken in a hurry.
> The hands that held electric charges
> now lie inert as four moored barges.
> The feet that ran to meet a date
> are running slow and running late.
> The eyes that shone and seldom shut
> are victims of a power cut.
> The parts that then transmitted joy
> are now reserved and cold and coy.

Romance, expected once to stay,
has left a note saying GONE AWAY.
    Gavin Ewart

13 *Night Crow*

When I saw that clumsy crow
Flap from a wasted tree,
A shape in the mind rose up:
Over the gulfs of dream
Flew a tremendous bird
Further and further away
Into a moonless black,
Deep in the brain, far back.
    Theodore Roethke

14 *Things to Come*

The shadow of a fat man in the moonlight
    Precedes me on the road down which I go;
And should I turn and run, he would pursue me:
    This is the man whom I must get to know.
    James Reeves

15 *Vitae Summa Brevis Spem Nos Vetat Incohare Longam*

They are not long, the weeping and the laughter,
    Love and desire and hate:
I think they have no portion in us after
    We pass the gate.

They are not long, the days of wine and roses:
    Out of a misty dream
Our path emerges for a while, then closes
    Within a dream.
    title: Life's short span forbids us to enter on far-reaching hopes. (Horace)
    Ernest Dowson

16 *Misguided Marcus*

Marcus met an alligator
Half a mile from the equator;
Marcus, ever optimistic,
Said, 'This beast is not sadistic.'
Marcus even claimed the creature

'Has a kind and loving nature'.
In that case, pray tell me, Marcus,
Why have you become a carcass?
   Colin West

17 *Shallow Poem*

I've thought of a poem.
I carry it carefully,
nervously, in my head,
like a saucer of milk;
in case I should spill some lines
before I can put them down.
   Gerda Mayer

18 *An Apology*

Owing to an increase
in the cost of printing
this poem will be less
than the normal length.

In the face of continued
economic crises, strikes,
unemployment and V.A.T.
it offers no solutions.

Moreover, because of
a recent work-to-rule
imposed by the poet
it doesn't even rhyme.
   Roger McGough

19 *Ants, although admirable, are awfully aggravating*

The busy ant works hard all day
And never stops to rest or play.
He carries things ten times his size,
And never grumbles, whines or cries.
And even climbing flower stalks,
He always runs, he never walks.
He loves his work, he never tires,
And never puffs, pants or perspires.

Yet though I praise his boundless vim
I am not really fond of him.
> *Walter R. Brooks*

20 *40 – Love*

middle	aged
couple	playing
ten–	nis
when	the
game	ends
and	they
go	home
the	net
will	still
be	be-
tween	them

> *Roger McGough*

Prayers are an integral part of all religions. They are used for thanking, for requesting, for promising and so on. Sometimes they use slightly old-fashioned words and phrases but these do not usually interfere with the message – and many prayers are expressed in everyday language.

Here you will find a selection taken from a variety of religions and traditions.

The Sample Text:
>God give me work
>Till my life shall end
>And life
>Till my work is done.
>>*Winifred Holtby*
>>*Novelist. 1898–1935*

1 EXPANSION
a) Add an extra line (or two lines) after line 1 and line 3.
>e.g. God give me work
>>*Which will help others as well as myself*
>>Till my life shall end
>>And life,
>>*Energy, good health and friends*
>>Till my work is done.

b) Insert adjectives in appropriate places.
>e.g. God give me *satisfying* work
>>Till my *earthly* life shall end
>>And *energetic* life
>>Till my *creative* work is done.

2 REDUCTION
Look at the prayer critically. Is it in fact possible to make it shorter? (Can you express 'Till my life shall end' more concisely?)
e.g. God give me work till I die and life to finish it.

3 MEDIA TRANSFER

a) Rewrite the prayer as a haiku (see p. 18).

> e.g. Lord let me have work
> till I die – and life until
> my work is finished

b) Rewrite the essence of the prayer as a journalist's report on part of an interview with the novelist.

> e.g. . . . she remarked that her work was very important to her. She prayed that there would always be interesting work for her to do and that . . .

4 MATCHING

Match the prayer with the saying below which best fits the prayer:
a) Some people live to work. Others work to live.
b) For some their work fits their life like a hand a glove.
c) Work expands to fill the time available for it. (Parkinson's Law)
d) The devil makes work for idle hands.
e) Let the work be sufficient unto the day.
f) Work is the curse of the drinking classes. (Oscar Wilde)

5 SELECTION/RANKING

a) Put the sayings in 4 (above) in order from most like to least like the message of the prayer.
b) Decide which of the purposes below would best be satisfied by the prayer, which next best etc. to least best.

i)   as a motto carved above an artist's studio door
ii)   as a mission statement for a charity organization involved with famine relief
iii) as the theme for a political speech on unemployment

6 COMPARISON/CONTRAST

Read these two texts. One is a poem, the other an epitaph.

a) My life is an hourglass;
> My work the sand that it contains.
> I pray you will not smash the glass
> Till no more sand remains.
>   *Alan Maley*

b) Here lies John Brown, a businessman,
> Cut off in his prime.
> He thought he could complete his business plan,
> But he ran out of time.
>   *Alan Maley*

Compare each of these with the prayer. In what ways are they similar/different? Do they contain the same language? The same ideas? The same images?

7 RECONSTRUCTION

Here are the words of a prayer. They are jumbled. Try to reconstruct the prayer using these words only.

give life (x2) work (x2) till (x2) and done is God me my (x2) shall end

8 REFORMULATION

a) Listen as your teacher reads this prayer twice. Here are three keywords from the prayer: life, work, time. Rewrite the prayer in your own words using the keywords to help you.

b) Imagine you know the person who wrote the prayer. You are telling another person about her. Write what you might say:
   e.g. Well, she used to say that . . .

c) Write a fragment of a radio interview with the novelist.
   e.g. Q. Can you tell us something about your attitude to work?
      A. Well, my work has always been very important to me. In fact . . .

9 INTERPRETATION

a) Was this prayer answered? (Look at it carefully again.)

b) Do you pray? Can you list the things you pray about?

c) Do you agree with the feelings expressed in this prayer?

d) Why do you think people pray? Is prayer useful?

10 CREATING TEXT

a) Take the theme of 'work' and write your own prayer. Exchange your prayer with your partner and try to improve it.

b) Write a prayer on any other theme which you feel strongly about. You may find it helpful to look at other prayers in this section before you start.

11 ANALYSIS

a) The text of the prayer is very economical. Check how many words are used more than once in it.

b) Yet 'Till my life shall end' is unnecessarily long. Can you suggest why it should use these five words when fewer could have been used? (e.g. Till I die. Till my life ends.) If you need a clue, look at the last line.

12 PROJECT WORK

a) In groups, prepare a questionnaire on 'attitudes to work'. You
should try to find out how important people think work is, what
kinds of work are most highly valued, when people should retire
etc.

When you have completed your questionnaire use it to collect
information from as many people as possible, including the other
members of the class. Tabulate the results and choose one member
of the group to give a short illustrated talk to the rest of the class.

b) Repeat the above procedure, taking 'attitudes to prayer' as the
topic of the inquiry.

Some further ideas

Try to set up some activities which involve looking through all the
texts before settling on particular ones for detailed attention. For
example:

a) Which is the most unusual prayer here?

b) Which is the funniest prayer?

c) Which prayer would you choose for yourself? Or for a friend?

d) Which is the simplest one to understand?

e) Which would be easiest to translate into your own language?

The activities which seem to work best with prayers are:

1 Expansion, 2 Reduction, 5 Selection/ranking, 6 Comparison/
contrast, 10 Creating text.

Prayers

1 In the beginning was God,
  Today is God,
  Tomorrow will be God.
  Who can make an image of God?
  He has no body.
  He is the word which comes out of your mouth.
  That word! It is no more,
  It is past, and still it lives!
  So is God.
      A Pygmy hymn

2 Lord,
  Keep my parents in your love.
  Lord,

bless them and keep them.
Lord,
please let me have money and strength
and keep my parents for many more years
so that I can take care of them.
Prayer of a young Ghanaian Christian

3 Lord, my heart is not large enough,
 my memory is not good enough,
 my will is not strong enough:
Take my heart and enlarge it,
Take my memory and give it quicker recall,
Take my will and make it strong
 and make me conscious of thee
 everpresent,
 ever accompanying.
 G.A.

4 God's thought in a man's brain,
God's love in a man's heart,
God's pain in a man's body,
 I worship.
 Margaret Cropper, 1886–1980

5 Lord, make me an instrument of your peace.
Where there is hatred, let me sow love,
Where there is injury, pardon;
Where there is doubt, faith;
Where there is despair, hope;
Where there is darkness, light;
Where there is sadness, joy.
O divine Master, Grant that I may not so much seek
To be consoled, as to console,
To be understood, as to understand,
To be loved, as to love,
For it is in giving that we receive;
It is in pardoning that we are pardoned;
It is in dying that we are born to eternal life.
 St Francis of Assisi, 1181–1226

6 Lord, take my lips and speak through them; take my mind and
 think through it; take my heart and set it on fire.
 W.H.H. Aitken

7 God be in my head, and in my understanding;
   God be in my eyes, and in my looking;
   God be in my mouth, and in my speaking;
   God be in my heart, and in my thinking;
   God be at my end, and at my departing.
     Old Sarum Primer

8 O Lord, thou knowest how busy I must be this day; if I forget
   thee, do not thou forget me: for Christ's sake.
     General Lord Astley (1579–1652), before the battle of Edgehill

9 – Night is drawing nigh –
   For all that has been – Thanks!
   For all that shall be – Yes!
     Dag Hammarskjöld, 1905–61

10 I have just hung up; why did he telephone?
   I don't know . . . Oh! I get it . . .
   I talked a lot and listened very little.
   Forgive me, Lord, it was a monologue and not a dialogue.
   I explained my idea and did not get his;
   Since I didn't listen, I learned nothing,
   Since I didn't listen, I didn't help,
   Since I didn't listen, we didn't communicate.
   Forgive me, Lord, for we were connected,
   and now we are cut off.
     Michel Quoist

11 O Lord, remember not only the men and women of good will,
   but also those of ill will. But do not remember all the suffering
   they have inflicted on us; remember the fruits we have bought,
   thanks to this suffering – our comradeship, our loyalty, our
   humility, our courage, our generosity, the greatness of heart
   which has grown out of all this, and when they come to
   judgement let all the fruits which we have borne be their
   forgiveness.
     *Prayer written by an unknown prisoner in Ravensbruck
     concentration camp and left by the body of a dead child*

12 *Right living*
   From the cowardice that dare not face new truth
   From the laziness that is contented with half truth

From the arrogance that thinks it knows all truth,
Good Lord, deliver me.
Prayer from Kenya

13 *Indian prayer*
From the unreal lead me to the real!
From darkness lead me to light!
From death lead me to immortality!
Brihad-Aranyaka Upanishad

14 Like an ant on a stick both ends of which are burning, I go to
and fro without knowing what to do and in great despair. Like
the inescapable shadow which follows me, the dead weight of
sin haunts me. Graciously look upon me. Thy love is my
refuge.
Source unknown

15 *The ten perfections*
I shall seek to develop the perfection of generosity, virtue,
doing without, wisdom, energy, forbearance, truthfulness,
resolution, love, serenity.

16 *Muslim prayer*
All that we ought to have thought, and have not thought,
All that we ought to have said, and have not said,
All that we ought to have done, and have not done;
All that we ought not to have thought, and yet have thought,
All that we ought not to have spoken, and yet have spoken,
All that we ought not to have done, and yet have done;
For thoughts, words and works, pray we, O god, for forgive-
ness.
From an ancient Persian prayer

17 *A grace from India*
Whatever I eat is of God, and from God,
and is mine as I am his.
(Rev. J.B. Gower)

18 *A Hebrew proverb*
He who eats and drinks, but does not bless the Lord, is a thief.

19 *Grace after pudding*
Bishop Burroughs, from Zimbabwe, relates how his mother
once said, 'I think we'll say grace after the meal – I am not
sure how the pudding will turn out.'

20 *Another short grace*
Bless these sinners as they eat their dinners.
    (J. Scott, Scargill House, N. Yorks)

21 *An appreciative grace*
Thanks for breakfast, lunch and dinner.
If it weren't for you, I'd be much thinner.
    (J. Stubbs)

22 *A grace from an American place-mat*
God of goodness, bless our food.
Keep us in a pleasant mood.
Bless the cook and all who serve us.
From indigestion, Lord, preserve us. Amen.

23 *A Christmas dinner from* Sketches by Boz *by Charles Dickens
(1812–70)*
Reflect upon your present blessings, of which every man has
many, not upon your past misfortunes, of which all men have
some.

24 *A guide grace*
Thank you for the meal before us spread,
For all those who worked to prepare it,
For the love that leads us to share it,
We thank you Lord, we thank you Lord.

25 Heavenly Father, bless us,
And keep us all alive;
There's ten of us to dinner
And not enough for five.

26 My God, bless this meal,
and give food to those who
have none.

27 Give me a good digestion, Lord,
   And also something to digest;
   But when and how that something comes
   I leave to thee, who knowest best.

28 Some hae meat, and canna eat
   And some wad eat that want it;
   But we hae meat and we can eat,
   And sae the Lord be thankit.

29 *A parachute regiment grace*
   Good food,
   Good friends,
   Safe landings,
   Thank God.

It is common to find brief descriptions of radio and TV programmes in daily newspapers and in special radio and TV magazines.

The Sample Text:

Antenna (8.10 p.m. BBC2)

The science magazine includes a report asking why there are so few boffins in our boardrooms while in the United States companies regularly promote scientists to management, on the assumption they will understand the importance of research. It amounts to another critical look at the divide between science and arts in British education, and a plea for closer collaboration between universities and industry.

The Independent on Sunday, 12 May 1991

I EXPANSION

In this text there are a number of insertion marks (↓). Select words from the list below to insert at the points indicated.

The ↓ science magazine includes a ↓ report asking why there are so few ↓ boffins in our ↓ boardrooms while in the United States ↓ companies regularly promote scientists to management ↓, on the ↓ assumption they will understand the importance of ↓ research. It amounts to another ↓ critical look at the ↓ divide between science and arts in ↓ British education, and a ↓ plea for closer collaboration between universities and ↓ industry.

current   severely   positions   British   topical   highly   critical
company   qualified   industrial   obvious   strong
yawning   commercial

2 REDUCTION

There are a number of words and phrases and one long clause which could be cut out of this text without losing the essential message. Find as many as you can and cut them (e.g. 'The science magazine', 'on the assumption . . . research', 'It amounts to' etc.).

3 MEDIA TRANSFER

a) Express the message of the text as a haiku (see p. 18.).

> e.g. in the USA.
> scientists are managers –
> not in the UK!

b) Make a visual representation of the structure of the information contained in the text.

> e.g.

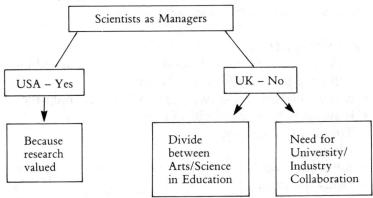

4 MATCHING

Match the text with the most suitable title:

a) Science and Industry
b) The Failings of British Education
c) Only Connect
d) Why No Scientists as Managers?

5 SELECTION/RANKING

a) Select a title for the text from among the words which make it up.

> e.g. Few Boffins in Our Boardrooms
> Scientists and Management

b) Look at the other programme details for the week of 12 May 1991 (see pp. 83–5). Decide which programme you would like to see most, which second-most etc., to the one you would like to see least.

6 COMPARISON/CONTRAST

Compare this letter to a newspaper with the text.

> Sir,
> I am appalled by the failures revealed in last Wednesday's 'Antenna' programme. To my mind this all goes back to British

snobbery. Education is regarded as a way of avoiding getting
your hands dirty. Anything to do with 'industry' is 'not an
occupation for gentlemen'. When will we learn, not only from
the States but from Japan, Germany and our other major com-
petitors? They don't seem to be obsessed with being educated
and idle!

     Yours sincerely . . .

What points does it make which are not in the programme details?
What points does it develop further?

7 RECONSTRUCTION

Here is a set of phrases and clauses. They are jumbled up. Try to
put them together to form a coherent text.

* closer collaboration between universities and industry
* It amounts to another critical look
* The science magazine
* asking why
* companies regularly promote scientists to management,
* includes a report
* there are so few boffins in our boardrooms
* while in the United States
* at the divide between science and arts in British education,
* they will understand
* and a plea for
* on the assumption
* the importance of research

8 REFORMULATION

Your teacher will read a text to you twice at normal speed. Make
notes on what you hear. Then rewrite the text using your notes.

9 INTERPRETATION

a) Is this a problem which you are familiar with in your country?
b) What do you think are the reasons for the 'divide' mentioned in
the notes?
c) What kinds of picture do you anticipate seeing in the programme?
How do you think the programme will be structured (e.g. introduction by the interviewer, some interviews in USA and UK
– in factories, corporate headquarters, universities, ministry of
education etc.).

10 CREATING TEXT

a) Here are some keywords from a text. Use them to write your own text. Then read the original text from which they were taken.

report science magazine why few boffins United States companies boardrooms scientists promote management research importance critical look the divide British education science and arts universities and industry a plea for closer collaboration

b) Decide on a similar problem to do with the management of industry in your own country. Then write a programme note for a TV programme on the subject.

11 ANALYSIS

a) Make lists of words to do with three key factors in the text: education, industry and science (e.g. boffins, science, scientists, research all relate to science).

b) Look at the structure of the text. The first sentence sets out a particular problem. The second sentence then relates this to two broader issues.

i.e. Specific issue → more general issues.

Look at the programme note on Public Eye: Choosing the Sex of Your Baby. Can you find an underlying structure there too?

c) Notice the way that many nouns are typically followed by a particular preposition in English. List the ones in this text (e.g. importance *of*, plea *for*, look *at*, collaboration *between*, divide *between* etc.). Look at the other texts in this section and see how many other examples you can find.

12 PROJECT WORK

In groups, find out as much as you can about the British education system. Then prepare a chart showing the various parts of the system from playschool to university.

Some further ideas

Try to set up some activities which involve looking at all the texts before starting to concentrate on any particular text. For example:

a) Look at all the programme notes and decide which programme you would like to watch.

b) Which programme would definitely not interest you?

c) Choose one of the programme notes on a subject which interests you. What do you already know about this topic? Make notes, then discuss them with a partner.

d) Do any of the programme notes deal with similar topics? (e.g. violence, the environment etc.)

The activities most suitable for use with programme notes include: 2 Reduction, 4 Matching, 5 Selection/ranking, 7 Reconstruction, 9 Interpretation, 11 Analysis.

Programme notes

The Icy Grave (Tuesday R4, 8.30pm) Eighty years ago tonight, the most luxurious liner ever built struck an iceberg on its maiden voyage. The *Titanic*, with its Adam fireplaces and Doric marbles, sank more than two miles to come to rest on the bottom of the Atlantic. More than 1,500 people lost their lives.

This 30-minute documentary is dignified and enthralling. It blends survivors' recollections, analysis of primitive navigation and insufficient lifeboats, and extraordinarily vivid testimony from the oceanographer Dr Robert Ballard, who located the ship on the ocean floor.

He talks of seeing a 'wall of steel like the gates of Troy', the chandeliers still hanging despite having fallen 12,000 feet, and his terror at catching sight of a porcelain doll's head outside the window of his submarine.

Most moving of all is his quiet description of all the pairs of shoes scattered among the debris on the seabed. The bodies were, of course, eaten, as were the clothes and skeletons, which also dissolved in the water. The shoes of 1912, however, were treated with tannic acid which fish dislike, which is why they all remain there to this day. 'Little children's shoes, women's shoes, I saw pairs of shoes all over the place . . .'

The Sunday Times,
12 April 1992

A Grief Observed (Friday R4, 11.25pm) In 1959, after three years of an intensely happy late marriage, the Christian scholar and author C.S. Lewis watched his wife, Joy, die of cancer. The way he chronicled his loss forms the basis of the West End play *Shadowlands*. One of the actors who played him, Nigel Hawthorne, now reads extracts from Lewis's journal in which, over many months, he journeyed with agonized honesty from 'the sudden jab of red-hot memories' and his torments over God as 'a cosmic sadist' to a more peaceful acceptance of the necessity of bereavement. Its themes of pain, despair, loss of faith and recovery of hope make this a most appropriate programme for Good Friday.

The Sunday Times,
12 April 1992

Film 91 With Barry Norman (10.30pm BBC1) Dirk Bogarde

reflects on his career of 60-plus films in this rare interview. He quit the UK for France in 1968, when the only work he was offered was a voice-over for a Forestry Commission film. Now back in London, the 70-year-old actor reveals how he has stayed at the top since first being a contract Rank star in 1947. 'I've never been greedy – I never earned what we call "Caine/Connery money" at all.' He is now promoting *These Foolish Things*, his first film for 12 years. The part he plays is semi-autobiographical – an ailing, yet dignified old man. 'I have no regrets. When I think I could have ended up like those thousands of retired businessmen who live in those dreary little bungalows outside Brighton, pottering about in their rain-drenched, gnome-ridden gardens, sipping their sherry or their Horlicks, waiting for the Nine O'Clock News on television, loathing all bloody foreigners, hating and mistrusting anything beyond their sceptr'd isle – when I think of that, it makes me ill.'

The Independent on Sunday,
12 May 1991

Inside Story (9.30pm BBC1)
Olivia Lichtenstein's documentary examines rape. One victim remembers it as though it were yesterday: 'When I finally got home, I went to bed and tried to sleep and couldn't. Every time I shut my eyes he was there. I could smell his breath. I just ending up screaming and screaming and screaming into my pillow.' The *Inside Story* cameras have been allowed into a special wing for sex offenders at Wayland Prison,

Norfolk. One rapist, 15 years into life sentence, observes: 'People tend to imagine that rape is purely a sex crime. It isn't, it's a crime of violence, violence against women.' Many women feel that they are to blame. They feel guilty and ashamed and are reluctant to go to court. Barrister Helena Kennedy says: 'We should be teaching our daughters to say "No" much more clearly and emphatically, and we should be teaching our sons to hear "No" and listen to it.'

The Independent on Sunday,
12 May 1991

Viewpoint 91 (10.40pm ITV) *Top Guns and Toxic Whales*, narrated by Anthony Hopkins, sounding disarmingly like Hannibal the Cannibal, contends that 'there is no more important form of security than environmental security. If we can't protect our environmental support systems, then there is no future for us.' This film, produced by Lawrence Moore and Robbie Stamp, winners of a Prix Italia for last year's *Can Polar Bears Tread Water?*, presents a depressing litany of statistics about environmental threats to global security. Every year an area of tropical rain forest the size of West Germany is destroyed. Egypt's thirsty population grows by one million every nine months. Forty thousand north Bohemian schoolchildren have to wear smog masks. Every year the United Nations allots a mere $18,000 to its environmental care programme, while $10bn is spent just on military satellite surveillance. Forces were immediately mobilized against

Iraq's invasion of Kuwait. Can we mobilize forces to protect the environment with the same urgency?

The Independent on Sunday,
12 May 1991

World in Action (8.30–9pm ITV)
Neil Charles is a businessman with no complaints about the state of the economy. As other companies struggle in the recession, he just doesn't want it to end. He is a pawnbroker, a man who has seen a 30 per cent increase in business this year. He is one person who has benefited from Britain's harsh economic climate. Jeff Anderson's film also meets: an insolvency expert who liquidates some of the 2,000 companies that collapse each month; an auctioneer who pockets a commission for selling some of the 4,000 repossessed homes each month; and a debt collector who chases some of the 45,000 people behind with payments.

The Independent on Sunday,
6 October 1991

Assignment (7.45–8.30pm BBC2)
BBC2's highly respected foreign affairs programme returns with an examination of the dangers posed by East Europe's nuclear power plants. Poorly designed and even more poorly maintained nuclear reactors are being abandoned by the Russians as they leave East Europe. With recent arms reduction treaties, the military threat is now being superseded by the disturbing prospect of nuclear disasters like Chernobyl.

The Independent on Sunday,
6 October 1991

Rough Justice (10.20–11.05pm BBC1) David Jessel presents *Murder or Mystery? The Curious Case of Baby Glen.* In 1988, 24-year-old Jacqueline Fletcher was convicted at Birmingham Crown Court of the murder of her six-week-old son. The question of murder arose after remarks Fletcher allegedly made within earshot of a neighbour. She was overheard saying to one of her children that she'd do to it what she'd done to the other. Steve Haywood's film discloses for the first time evidence that Fletcher is mentally handicapped, incapable of understanding the implications of what she was saying, or the confession of murder she was subsequently to make. The programme claims that had Fletcher's mental vulnerability been known, her confession might not have been accepted as evidence in court. Rough Justice continues to boldly go where no lawyer has gone before.

The Independent on Sunday,
3 November 1991

Screen Two: The Count of Solar (10.10pm BBC2) The Abbé de l'Epée, enlightened inventor of sign language, undertakes to train an abandoned deaf and dumb boy. At first, David Nokes's screenplay seems like a rehash of François Truffaut's *The Wild Child*; then the Abbé discovers that the boy may have a claim to a title. David Calder and Tyron Woolfe star in a thoughtful study of *noblesse oblige*, soberly designed, directed by Tristram Powell.

Fragile Earth: Caviar (7pm C4)
All Russia's caviar belongs to the state, but the people of the Volga have long taken their tithe of the harvest. But recently illegal poaching has attracted organized crime and the river is said to be on the brink of an ecological catastrophe from industrial pollution. This informative documentary is enlivened by folkloric scenes of dancing peasants and archive footage of Stalin inaugurating the electrification programmes of the Thirties. The commentary was apparently written before Leningrad changed its name.

The Independent on Sunday,
2 February 1992

Mister Johnson (*PG; Curzon, Phoenix*). Joyce Cary's novel, set in pre-war Nigeria, tells the story of a clash of values between a sympathetic district officer (Pierce Brosnan) and his native clerk (Maynard Eziashi), who is determined to be more English than his colonial masters. Eziashi gives a moving performance and Bruce Beresford's film, though accused of stereotyping, is a sincere exploration of colonial attitudes.

The Independent on Sunday,
21 April 1992

Citizen Kane (*U; Curzon Phoenix, Plaza Piccadilly*). Orson Welles's first and best film is 50 years old, making a happy return for a limited season to the West End. All that depth and richness of image, keeping company with a tale of vain trappings and superficial power: Welles's telling of a tycoon's life, from damaged boyhood to lonely death, has never looked more pertinent, or more fun.

The Independent on Sunday,
21 April 1992

Critical Eye (9–10pm C4) Channel 4's polemical documentary series ends tonight with a double bill. Rebecca Doobs's *Operation Solstice* recounts the story of the arrest of 420 people on their way to the Free Peoples' Festival at Stonehenge on 1 June 1985. In the longest-running civil case in British legal history, 24 of them sued the police for damages. In February, many claims for assault and false imprisonment were upheld. *The Battle for Orgreave: The Sequel*, produced by Vanson Wardle, also examines police action in the mid-Eighties. This investigation into the 1984 Orgreave conflict interviews miners who earlier this year won compensation totalling almost half a million pounds from the police. One miner reveals how the battle has changed him: 'You are always brought up to trust the police . . . but now I have nothing to do with them.'

The Independent on Sunday,
30 June 1992

Short Stories (8.30pm C4) Juliet Darling's *A Pair of One*, the most remarkable programme of the week, looks at Greta and Freda Chaplin, an inseparable pair of twins. Having lived together for 48 years, the twins now talk in unison, dress the same, even walk in step. If separated for a moment, they become hysterical. They avoid crowds, as they attract ridicule. They insist on having the same amount of food on their plates, and they eat their chips at exactly the same second. If the telephone rings, both will have the same conversation, one after the other. The twins' obsession with uniformity extends to buying the same size shoes, even though Greta has larger feet. Every two weeks they take the train to York where they stand outside their parents' house hoping for a glimpse. Their parents, however, will not see them. The twins are trapped in one mind, a single identity in two people. 'We feel like we're one person, not two people. If doing everything together causes problems, we don't see it.'

James Rampton
The Independent on Sunday,
19 May 1992

Public Eye (8–8.30pm BBC2)
Choosing the Sex of Your Baby – Unnatural Selection asks whether parents should be able to select the sex of their child. American doctor Ron Ericsson thinks they should, and is planning to introduce his sex-selection techniques to Britain. Dr Ericsson has become a millionaire through licensing his method of sex selection, known as 'sperm separation'. This involves dividing the male-determining Y sperm from the female-determining X chromosome sperm and then artifically inseminating with the required type. The technique is safe, easy and relatively cheap, and its inventor claims a success rate of around 80 per cent. The ultimate in consumer choice or just meddling with nature?

James Rampton
The Independent on Sunday,
3 November 1991

The mini-saga is a story which must be told in exactly *fifty* words. The best mini-sagas have an unexpected or clever ending.

Mini-sagas were first developed in competitions run by the *Daily Telegraph* between 1982 and 1987.

The Sample Text:

THE INNER MAN
Their marriage was
a perfect union of trust
and understanding. They
shared everything – except
his desk drawer, which,
through the years remained
locked.
One day, curiosity
overcame her. Prised open,
there was – nothing.
'But why?' she asked,
confused and ashamed.
'I needed a space of my
own,' he replied sadly.
Christine M. Banks

1 EXPANSION
a) Make the following additions to the text:
  • after 'They shared everything' give examples of the things they shared (e.g. their interests, their tastes, their friends, their holidays . . .).
  • after 'overcame her' insert a sentence about how she felt about her action.
   e.g. She wondered what secret it might contain.
  • – after 'nothing' write a sentence filling in the time between her action and her conversation with her husband.
   e.g. Later on, when she had plucked up courage to tell her husband what she had done, . . .
b) Write a paragraph before the text, which sets the scene for the

story, and a paragraph at the end of the text, which tells us how the story ended, what the consequences of her action were. Everyone should contribute their ideas in a full class discussion.

2 REDUCTION

a) Reduce the text to a one-word title. The word must occur in the text (e.g. Curiosity, Trust, Space etc.).
b) Rewrite the story using only forty words or less. Work with a partner, then share your ideas with another pair.

3 MEDIA TRANSFER

a) Transfer the information in the text into a short article for the local newspaper. The headline of the article will be 'Local couple divorces'. Work in groups of four and post up your articles for other groups to read.
b) Write a haiku (see p.18) based on the information in the mini-saga.
   e.g. they shared everything
            except his locked desk drawer –
      whose guilty secret?

4 MATCHING

a) On page 89 are pictures of three married couples. Which one matches best with your idea of the couple in the text? Explain the reasons for your choice to your partner.
b) Here are three paraphrases of the moral of the text. Which one fits your understanding of the text best?
   i)   Suspicion is a dangerous thing.
   ii)   Nobody is perfect.
   iii) Everybody needs privacy some of the time.

5 SELECTION

a) Select a phrase from the text which best sums up its meaning (e.g. 'a space of my own', 'curiosity overcame her').
b) Here are two texts. Which one do you think was the original and which one was the copy?
   i)   Their marriage was a perfect union of trust and understanding. They shared everything – except his desk drawer, which through the years remained locked. One day, curiosity overcame her. Prised open, there was – nothing. 'But why?' she asked, confused and ashamed. 'I needed a space of my own,' he replied sadly.
   ii)   They had a perfect marriage. They trusted each other totally.

Everything they had, they shared – except his desk drawer, which he always kept locked. She became so curious that one day she broke it open. It was empty. She felt ashamed. 'I needed a space of my own,' he explained.

6 COMPARISON/CONTRAST
'Curiosity killed the cat' is a well-known proverb. Can you think of stories you know which show the problems that excessive curiosity can cause? (e.g. *The Sorcerer's Apprentice, Pandora's Box*)

7 RECONSTRUCTION
a) This text has a number of gaps. Fill them with words you think are appropriate:

Their marriage was a perfect _____ of trust and _____. They shared everything _____ his desk drawer, which through the _____ remained _____. One _____, curiosity _____ her. Prised open, there was _____. 'But why?' she _____, confused and _____. 'I needed a _____ of my own,' he replied _____.

Check your version with your partner's.

b) The sentences in this text are in the wrong order. Put them back into an order you think makes sense. There is also a sentence which should not be there. Decide which one it is and leave it out. Work in pairs and compare your version with another pair when you have finished.

One day, curiosity overcame her. They shared everything – except his desk drawer, which through the years remained locked. 'But why?' she asked, confused and ashamed. Their marriage was a perfect union of trust and understanding. She looked everywhere for the key, which she was sure he had hidden. 'I needed a space of my own,' he replied sadly. Prised open, there was – nothing.

8 REFORMULATION
a) Read this text once. Then put it away. Retell the story to your group in your own words.

b) Read the text once. Put it away. Then use these keywords from it to rewrite your own version of the story.

Keywords: marriage trust shared desk drawer locked curiosity open nothing why? ashamed space sadly

Compare your version with your neighbour's.

9 INTERPRETATION

a) What would *you* have done if you had been the wife? And the husband? Note it down, then your teacher will ask you to contribute to the class discussion.

b) What questions would you like to ask the wife? And the husband? Make a list, then discuss what the answers might have been with your partner.

c) Does the story remind you of any incidents in your own life, of people you have known or stories you have heard? Tell the class.

10 CREATING TEXT

a) Choose ten words from the text. Then use them to write a completely different story. Display your stories on the class notice-board.

b) Use the text as a model but change the topic.

e.g. Their home was a perfect example of happiness and fulfilment. They enjoyed everything – except the weekends, which through the years remained depressing. One day, despair overcame him. He left home . . .

11 ANALYSIS

a) Make a list of all the words in the text which relate to human feelings (e.g. trust, understanding, curiosity, shame, confusion, sadness).

b) Which of the following are the best equivalents for the words in the text (in context)?

- union – bond, combination, fusion, blend
- prised open – broken open, eased open, forced open, blown open
- ashamed – guilty, blameworthy, self-conscious, culpable
- shared – divided, co-operated, partnership, jointly owned
- space – area, place, secret, void

Check your choices with your teacher.

12 PROJECT WORK

In groups of four, construct a questionnaire designed to discover people's attitudes to the subject of trust between people. It might be phrased in questions like 'Have you ever . . .?' (e.g. Have you ever opened/read someone else's letters?) or 'Would you . . .?' (e.g. Would you tell your girlfriend if you had been out with someone else?).

Ask class members to complete the questionnaire, then tabulate the results. Are there significant differences between male and female attitudes?

Some further ideas

To help students become familiar with the full range of texts in this section, ask them to browse through them. Possible activities include:

a) Choose one mini-saga you like the look of. You should read it carefully and prepare to retell it from memory, either to your partner or to your group.

b) In pairs, choose another text you find interesting and write a series of questions on it. These should be genuine questions, i.e. things you really want to know about the story. Your pair then joins another pair. The texts and questions are exchanged and you speculate about, and discuss, what the answers might be.

The activities which work best with mini-sagas are:

1 Expansion, 3 Media transfer, 6 Comparison/contrast, 8 Reformulation, 9 Interpretation.

Mini-sagas

THE

DEATH TOUCH

When a daughter went
away to college, she reluctantly
left her plants and her
goldfish in her mother's care.
Once the daughter telephoned
and her mother confessed
that the plants and
the goldfish had died.
There was a prolonged silence.
Finally, in a small voice,
the daughter asked,
'How's Dad?'
Dawn Hunt

THE PURSUIT OF

YOUTH

The blonde and her
young student lover lived

together in his bedsitter.
She regarded the mirror
and worried. With fear in
her heart, she shopped every
lunch-hour, until their
room was stacked with lipsticks,
shoes and dresses.
One evening, opening the
wardrobe, she failed to see
his suit was gone.

Suzi Robinson

IN THE BEST CIRCLES
LOVE WILL FIND A WAY TO
ENCOMPASS TRIANGLES

By the young Countess's
grave her lover bowed his
head and wept uncontrollably.
For seven years, her ageing
husband turning a discreet
blind eye, he had shared
her favours. The Count laid
an encouraging arm across
his shoulders. 'Do not
despair, my friend.
I promise you, I
shall marry again.'

Eve Jennings

THE BLIND OLD LADY

They spoke loudly
and slowly to her, as if
her ears and brain were worn
out too. Guiding her here
and there, moving this
and fetching that. Being
there – but always just out
of reach, lest she cling
to them, lest she needed more
than duty . . . lest she
needed love.

Susan E. Thorpe

MEN WHO LIVE IN
MUD HOUSES . . .
How the tribe laughed
when the anthropologist
couldn't recognize his own
camel among their herd,
even reminding him
of it as they
waved goodbye.
And when he returned, how
the tribe greeted him
and delighted in telling
him the story of the white
man who couldn't recognize
his own camel . . .
Jonathan Hall

RELATIVE VALUES
Mrs Newgood cared.
She cared for the Earth,
the welfare of its peoples
and its wildlife. She fought
to ban the Bomb, nuclear
power, acid rain, meat eating,
smoking and any alcohol but
wine. She cared for
Mr Everight who espoused
her causes. Her husband
was left holding the baby.
Michael Brightley

STATUS REPORT CRAFT # 391:
SUBJECT EARTH
Intelligent lifeform smaller than
anticipated and extremely
delicate. They are in the early
stages of development, but
unfortunately have stumbled
upon nuclear physics. Global
self-destruction imminent;
re-industrialization, several
hundred years hence. They
are an unimportant species,
and pose no immediate
threat save to themselves.
Suggest we ignore.
Over.
John Kirkbride

CARELESS LOVE
The kettle sang from the
kitchen as she quickly tidied
round the room, occasionally
looking toward the door. Today
he would come, and there would
be laughter and talk. Her
grandson loved her stories.
The day moved on, he didn't
even phone. Three times that
week the kettle boiled dry.
Caroline Ward

In English newspapers there is usually at least one column of short news stories. These are sometimes called Stop Press – stories which come in too late for a long article to be written on them. But there are also stories which usually have a human-interest side, which would not merit longer treatment. These are sometimes amusing.

The Sample Text:

Doctors in a Hurry

Waving a stethoscope while speeding to indicate the urgency of their mission is not the best way for doctors to avoid being stopped by the police, according to a report in *The Lancet*. Two doctors hurtling along the motorway to an emergency case did just this when they saw a police car keeping level with them in the outside lane. The uniformed occupants responded by dangling a pair of handcuffs out of the window to tell the medics to pull over.

Fortunately, there was a happy ending: the doctors explained themselves and were provided with a police escort for the rest of their journey.

I EXPANSION

a) Try to add the following adverbs to the text (either just before or just after a verb).

immediately (x2) persuasively blithely abruptly headlong illegally suggestively completely helpfully

e.g. *Blithely* waving a stethoscope . . .

b) Write a brief paragraph which could have preceded this article and one which could be added at the end.

e.g. No one is above the law – not even the medical profession, as the following incident shows . . .

However, doctors have been warned by the BMA (British Medical Association) that in future . . .

2 REDUCTION

Remove six phrases/clauses which can be cut without seriously affecting the meaning (e.g. 'to indicate the urgency of their mission', 'according to a report in *The Lancet*' etc.).

3 MEDIA TRANSFER

a) Write the incident out as a letter from one of the doctors to a
friend.

   e.g. Dear Jim,
        Peter and I had a brush with the police last week. We'd
        been called out to an emergency following a pile-up on the
        motorway . . .

b) Write the incident out as it might have been recorded in the
policeman's report.

   e.g. 7 p.m. We were passed by a Renault 25 travelling at 100 mph
        on the M6 motorway between exits 21 and 22. We gave
        chase and drew alongside . . .

4 MATCHING

On page 98 are three visual presentations of the events described.
Which one matches best with the text?

5 SELECTION/RANKING

a) Put these sayings in order according to how well they fit the sense
of the article.
   • More haste, less speed.
   • Time and tide wait for no man.
   • A stitch in time saves nine.
   • There's a time and place for everything.
   • The Future is something which everyone reaches at the rate of
     60 minutes an hour, whatever he does, whoever he is. (C.S.
     Lewis)
   • He who hesitates is lost.

b) Which of these titles fits the article best, which next best and
which least well?
   • Emergency Stop
   • Road Signs
   • Fast Aid!

6 COMPARISON/CONTRAST

Here are two limericks dealing with the subject of doctors/driv-
ing/the police:

   There was a young doctor called Hall
   On her way to a fancy-dress ball.
   After drinks in a bar
   She sped in her car.

A

B

C

Said the policeman, 'This won't do at all!'
Alan Maley

All medics are reckless young men.
It's been proven again and again:
They drive far too fast,
Get arrested at last,
And imprisoned for five years (or ten).
Alan Maley

Compare the information in the limericks with that in the article. Which items are common, which different?

7 RECONSTRUCTION

These sentences are in the wrong order. Rearrange them to form a text which makes sense.

- Two doctors hurtling along the motorway to an emergency case did just this when they saw a police car keeping level with them in the outside lane.
- Fortunately, there was a happy ending: the doctors explained themselves and were provided with a police escort for the rest of their journey.
- Waving a stethoscope while speeding to indicate the urgency of their mission is not the best way for doctors to avoid being stopped by the police, according to a report in *The Lancet*.
- The uniformed occupants responded by dangling a pair of handcuffs out of the window to tell the medics to pull over.

8 REFORMULATION

a) Your teacher will read you a short newspaper article twice. Take careful notes, then use the notes to rewrite the article in your own words.
b) Rewrite the article reversing the order of information in each sentence.
   e.g. According to a report in *The Lancet* . . .
      When they saw a police car . . .
      In order to tell the medics to pull over . . .
      The doctors explained . . .
      . . . so there was a happy ending.

9 INTERPRETATION

a) What is the popular image of doctors in your country? And medical students?

b) Can you think of any incidents involving doctors in brushes with the law?

c) Draw a cartoon sequence to illustrate the incident.

d) What questions would you put to the doctors in this incident? And to the police?

10 CREATING TEXT

Write a new text in the form of a short article with the same title – Doctors in a Hurry – but with a different content (e.g. an incident in which doctors left a swab inside a patient after an operation because they had a long list of people waiting etc.).

11 ANALYSIS

a) What does 'just this' refer to in line 4?

b) Find synonyms or equivalent paraphrases of the following words in the text:

doctors
police
emergency case
speeding
waving

c) See Reformulation b), above. Why is the order of information in each sentence the way it is and not reversed, although it makes sense either way?

12 PROJECT WORK

a) In groups, design a questionnaire to find out people's attitudes towards the medical profession – both positive and negative. Use the questionnaire to collect information from as many people as you can, then present your findings to the whole class.

b) Plan a visit to your local newspaper office with a view to finding out as much as you can about how the news is chosen, and what happens to it before it finally appears in the newspaper. You will need to plan your questions very carefully.

Some further ideas

Give the students the opportunity to look at all the articles before you choose one to work on in more depth. The following activities are possible:

a) Which headline do you find most effective? Discuss your ideas with your partner.
b) Which article did you find most interesting? Why?
c) Which article was the most unusual?
The activities which work best with short newspaper articles are:
1 Expansion, 2 Reduction, 3 Media transfer, 8 Reformulation, 9 Interpretation, 11 Analysis.

Short newspaper articles

Dustmen find family fortune

DUSTMEN have returned 10 million yen (£42,550) which was accidentally thrown out with the rubbish.

A couple living in central Tokyo had hidden their savings in an old chest of drawers. When they realized what they had done, they called the police, who said the money had already been handed in.

A police spokesman said: 'This is a barometer of how safe Japan is. In other countries, the cash probably would not have been returned.'

The Evening Standard,
17 June 1992

Small victory

Versailles (AP) – A court yesterday paved the way for the return of dwarf-tossing in France. It rescinded an order that barred Manuel Wackenheim from being tossed on to a mattress at a nightclub and fined Morsang-sur-Orge, the town that imposed the ban, 10,000 francs (£1,000). Mr Wackenheim, known as 'Mr Skyman', said the ban was an attack on individual liberty and his right to work.

The Independent,
26 February 1992

Not goofy

PARENTS concerned that their children's thumb- or finger-sucking will damage their teeth and leave them permanently goofy should relax. Although two-thirds of toddlers suck their thumbs, fingers or some other comforter, and more than half of six-year-olds occasionally suck their fingers, there is no evidence to suggest that this behaviour leads to facial deformity – but the front teeth of children over the age of eight who are chronic suckers do stick out. However, even when sucking stops as late as 10, the teeth usually return to the right position.

An editorial in *The Lancet* points out that while a device can be fitted to a child's teeth to prevent sucking, there is little point when most children give up the habit spontaneously. Moreover, these devices can be uncomfortable and may put children off so much that they refuse to co-operate when they need orthodontic treatment.

Olivia Timbs
The Independent,
21 April 1992

The Barbican Blues

The Bank of England looks to have

solved the problem of disposing of 2,000 tonnes of shredded banknotes each year. The notes, worth billions of pounds, will be used to make garden compost to plant trees at the Botanic Centre in Acklam, Middlesbrough.

Who was it who said that money does not grow on trees?

The Independent,
31 August 1990

Fishy cocktails
Wellington (AFP) – A bar has run into trouble for serving cocktails with live goldfish in them. The Society for the Prevention of Cruelty to Animals is investigating three complaints that Route 66 serves Goldfish Laybacks – tequila and lemon plus a live goldfish.

The Independent,
9 March 1992

Colas banned
Singapore (Reuter) – Sugary soft drinks such as Coca-Cola and Pepsi will be banned from sale in Singapore schools from June, the *Straits Times* newspaper said yesterday. The aim is to promote a healthy lifestyle and reduce obesity among students, an Education Ministry spokesman said.

The Independent,
23 April 1992

Miracle cure
Algiers (AFP) – An Algerian who lost his voice after five men beat him and threatened to kill him has been cured with whisky, the *El Watan* daily reported.

Doctors could do nothing for Ziane Bensahli, 28. But villagers suggested whisky. 'On the ninth day, he was able to talk again. First noises, then whispers, then words,' the paper said.

The Independent,
15 April 1992

Stomaching the truth
From Ms Veronica Piekosz
Sir: Last Saturday I was amused to be told that pre-school children don't equate animals with meat ('Where do Moo cows go when they die?', 25 April).

We have a traditional butcher with his own slaughterhouse in this village and I have never hidden from my children the facts of life and death. On seeing a load of beasts (cattle) in a lorry my three-year-old daughter remarked 'Mr Robinson will have to take off all that black and white skin before we can eat those cows.'
Yours sincerely,
VERONICA PIEKOSZ
Great Smeaton,
North Yorkshire
29 April

The Independent,
1 May 1992

Horse surprise
Jerusalem (Reuter) – Tourists and police at the Israeli resort of Eilat were surprised by a visitor from King Hussein's palace in Aqaba – an Arabian gelding which swam to Israel. The horse was checked to see if it was booby-trapped.

The Independent,
8 April 1992

Revenge is sweet
From Mr P.C. Mitchell

Sir: I enjoy elections. For four years the politicians have bullied us, taxed us and generally given us a bad time. Now, for four weeks, we have them at our mercy. They roll on their backs like trained seals, clapping their flippers, wear red noses and kiss ugly babies.

I really enjoy elections. Oh yes!

Yours faithfully,
MIKE MITCHELL
Manchester
3 April

In sincere praise of older parents
From Ms Helen Griffiths

Sir: Monica Neville's sympathy (letter, 20 February) for children with older parents is misplaced. Both my parents were a few months short of their 40th birthdays when I was born in 1965, and this never impeded my education or made me feel ashamed of their age.

During the power cuts of the early Seventies my mother, having survived air raids and rationing, coped far better than our more youthful neighbours.

Yours sincerely,
HELEN GRIFFITHS
Morden Park, Surrey
20 February

From Ms Susan Gill

Sir: I feel well equipped to answer Monica Neville's letter (20 February) about children with older parents, as my mother was 35 when I was born, my father 50.

Far from causing me embarrassment, my parents' age was a source of great pride to me at school: they were so much older than anyone else's! The only difficulty I ever experienced was when my father began to slow down as I was speeding up. When walking together, the problem was easily solved by taking his arm, a habit I retained until he died when I was 21.

Those 21 years I regard as being blessed. At retirement age my mother greets life as she always has, with smiling grace. I am perfectly satisfied with my role models.

Yours faithfully,
SUSAN GILL
Oxford
20 February

The Independent,
4 April 1992

Children on aircraft 'get a raw deal'

CHILDREN are getting a raw deal on aircraft, in hotels and on holidays, according to a report published today. Airlines are the biggest culprits, providing 'woefully inadequate' facilities, *Good Holiday* magazine said.

'Some airlines even ban children from first class, or, if they are in first class and start crying, require them to move to economy class and cry there,' said its editor, John Hill.

The magazine said airlines charged for babes in arms that weighed no more than hand luggage and provided so few facilities for children that they got up and played in dangerous areas.

These included playing near the toilets (unhygienic, and blocks the aisles); near the kitchen (danger of scalding) and at the emergency exits where they twiddle with locks and gave passengers 'near heart attacks'.

The magazine said some British holiday companies did not take children and that Britain appeared to be the most discriminating country over children. Top countries for looking after children are France, Spain and the Mediterranean countries.

The Independent,
24 February 1992

Cheers

Fewer Frenchmen die of heart attacks than Scotsmen. Now French scientists have discovered it is because wine is much better for you than Scotch. An ideal regimen suggests itself: a long walk in the heather before breakfast, then a hearty bowl of porridge – no salt, of course – accompanied by a decent Margaux '81.

The Evening Standard,
9 June 1992

Pricey dust-ups

Taipei (AFP) – Scuffles between deputies at Taiwan's National Assembly in the past 10 days have cost taxpayers almost 50m Taiwan dollars (£1.2m) in lost time, an official said. The cost of furniture damaged when the deputies jumped on it and microphones they ripped out has yet to be calculated.

The Independent,
30 March 1992

Loser by a nose

Lagos (AFP) – A Nigerian professor has been jailed for a year after biting the nose of a student whom he saw with one of his two wives,

the official Nigerian news agency, Nan, reported.

Nan said the professor, Apollo Jallo, 36, attacked Hussaini Danjuma, 23, when he saw the student walking with his wife Esther last March in a small town near Jos.

The professor, who is about to become a father for the 13th time, was also fined 1,000 naira (£65).

The Independent,
3 September 1991

More smokers are giving up

ONLY three in 10 people now smoke, Government figures show. Just 31 per cent of men and 29 per cent of women over 16 lit up last year compared with 52 per cent and 41 per cent in 1972.

But the study by the Health Education Authority also says more youngsters are starting. And a report out on Monday warned that tobacco is killing 300 Britons a day.

The Daily Mirror,
27 November 1991

I was the Loch Ness Monster

This is the picture of Nessie that started the world's monster mania.

But now, 58 years after it was snapped by London surgeon Robert Wilson, a former music teacher has come forward to claim: 'I was the Monster.'

Lambert Wilson, 86, who is not related to the photographer, says he decided to break his silence after seeing the picture reprinted in the *Daily Mail* on August 12 alongside a new Loch Ness Monster photograph taken by an anonymous reader.

Wilson was working as conductor

at His Majesty's Theatre in Aberdeen when he decided to pull the stunt, he says. 'I got a serpent's head from a joke shop and with some help from the theatrical costumiers made my own monster head and neck with a tiny peephole so that I could see.'

Mr Wilson, of Beaufort Road, Morecambe, said he knew the times coach parties would stop at the loch.

'I was there for about 15 minutes, gliding through the water very gently,' he said.

'Through the peephole I could make out people on shore pointing and taking pictures. At one stage I got so close that they tried to throw stones at me.'

Mr Wilson, a keen swimmer at the time, said he carried out the stunt to test the gullibility of the public. 'I certainly fooled a lot of people for a long time,' he said.

The Daily Mail,
22 August 1992

Bank heroine walks out on raider

BANK clerk Julia Macklin came face to face with a masked gunman yesterday – and calmly turned her back on him.

'I'll shoot you,' he yelled but, slowly and steadily, she strode out into the street, then dashed to a phone box to dial 999. Minutes later a police helicopter was hovering above the TSB in Stretford, Manchester, and the building was surrounded by armed officers.

For three hours police laid siege to the bank and then burst in – only to find the robber had fled, empty-handed. He is believed to have escaped through a window at the rear as soon as the 23-year-old clerk walked out on him.

The thief, who climbed in through the roof, was waiting when Mrs Macklin opened the bank. He demanded keys to the safe.

When she told him she didn't have them, he 'warned her of the consequences if she didn't do what she was told.' But Mrs Macklin – a 'remarkable, extremely brave lady', said police – called his bluff.

The Daily Mail,
4 April 1992

Would you credit it?

HOW carefully do you check your credit card statement every month? Normally I glance over the items very briefly before lingering painfully on the total amount to be paid.

However, checking my statement this month, I noticed two items for meals at the same restaurant in Italy. The first meal cost £332.47; the second, £171.47. Somebody clearly had a good time – unfortunately it wasn't me. I have not been to Italy for nearly 18 months.

I telephoned Trustcard immediately and informed them that the restaurant bills had nothing to do with me. After some initial scepticism ('Are you sure you didn't give your credit card to anybody?'), Trustcard accepted my assurances and agreed to set these items aside pending further investigation.

The company informed me that, as a further safeguard, my account would carry a flag, so that if my card was used in Italy again the person using it would be asked my date of birth to make sure that it was really me.

The situation is, however, a worrying one. My card has never been stolen, so how did these two items end up on my bill? Trustcard's press office suspected some sort of fraud; credit card fraud is a big growth industry, particularly in Italy. In the UK, fraud with all types of plastic card accounted for a loss of £120m in 1990, rising last year by 35 per cent to £165m.

According to the Credit Card Research Group, such fraud is so advanced a science in the Far East that you can hand your card to a waiter and, by the time he has returned with the slip for you to sign, someone in a backroom will have made a perfect copy.

Never let your credit card out of your sight, I was told: always accompany the waiter who takes your card to the cash desk. Easier said than done.

However, this still does not explain how two Italian restaurant bills managed to appear on my credit card statement.

If any other readers have had similar experiences, I would be very interested to hear about them.

Frank Barrett
The Independent,
11 April 1992

The Mulla Nasruddin (also known as the Hodja) is a favourite character who figures in a large number of stories and fables from Turkey, Iran and other parts of the Middle East. He is traditionally depicted as a kind of wise fool and many of the stories are paradoxical or apparently absurd. For Sufi Muslims, the stories are used as a way of 'opening up' the mind and spirit.

The Sample Text:
One day Nasruddin was expecting some guests for supper, so he bought some goat's meat for his wife to cook. When the guests had arrived, his wife served lots of vegetable dishes but no meat – she had already eaten it herself.

'Where's the meat?' inquired Nasruddin.

'The cat ate it – all three pounds of it,' replied his wife.

Nasruddin called for some scales, then weighed the cat. It weighed exactly three pounds.

'There seems to be a slight problem,' said Nasruddin. 'If this is the cat, then where is the meat? And if this is the meat, then what has happened to the cat?'

I EXPANSION
a) Add as many adjectives as you can to the text, e.g. . . . some *important* guests, some *delicious, fresh* goat's meat etc.
b) Add as many of these adverbs as you can at appropriate points in the text:
innocently solemnly anxiously greedily carefully obediently nonchalantly

e.g. 'Where's the meat?' Nasruddin inquired *nonchalantly*.
c) Insert sentences at appropriate points in the text, which comment or give more information on what is happening.

e.g. . . . wife to cook. *Now his wife was an extremely greedy woman and when she saw the meat she just couldn't resist it.* When the guests . . . eaten it herself. *Nasruddin was somewhat worried by the absence of the meat but he tried not to show it* . . . etc.
d) Write a paragraph which introduces the story and one which rounds it off.

e.g. Nasruddin and his wife were always quarrelling about something. Often it was his wife's greedy habits which led to an
argument.

. . .

'No problem,' said his wife, 'since he ate the meat he's been
on a diet.'

2 REDUCTION
Shorten the story any way you can without losing its essential
meaning.
e.g. Nasruddin, expecting some guests, bought goat's meat for
supper. At supper his wife only served vegetable dishes however . . .

3 MEDIA TRANSFER
Use the story, including the parts which are already in dialogue,
to write a sketch.
e.g. NAS. I'm expecting some guests this evening, dear. Here's
three pounds of goat meat to prepare a stew.
WIFE All right, dear. (aside) Greedy old fool. It looks
delicious. I think I'll have it myself . . .

4 MATCHING
Choose the proverb or saying below which best matches the
meaning of the fable.
• When the cat's away the mice will play.
• You can't have one without the other.
• You can't have it both ways.
• Now you see it, now you don't.
• She let the cat out of the bag.
• You can't have your cake and eat it.

5 SELECTION/RANKING
Choose the best title from the list below. Then put the others in
order from most suitable to least suitable.
• Scales of Justice
• A Weighty Matter
• Scapegoat
• Where's It Gone?
• Vanishing Trick
• The Meat of the Argument
• The Goat, the Cat and the Wife

6 COMPARISON/CONTRAST

Compare the fable with these stories in terms of the following keywords:

    honesty cunning wisdom weighing flesh/blood
    contradiction

- King Solomon was reputed to be very wise. One day two women came to him with a baby. Both of them claimed to be its mother. Neither would yield the baby to the other. Eventually King Solomon gave his judgment: 'Let the baby be cut in half and half given to each woman.' At this one of the women cried out, 'No. Let the other woman keep him. I can't bear to see him killed.' King Solomon then said, 'Give the baby to *this* woman who is obviously his true mother.'

- The Sultan wanted to find a totally honest Finance Minister so he arranged a competition. Before they came in, each candidate was left alone in a room full of precious stones and gold coins in baskets. Then, when they came before the Sultan, they were asked to dance for five minutes. The first ten candidates proved to be very poor dancers; they could hardly lift their feet off the ground. But the eleventh was splendid – leaping and whirling around. The Sultan immediately chose him as Finance Minister. The others were taken away and executed.

7 RECONSTRUCTION

Complete the gaps in this text with the words or phrases which you think are missing.

e.g. One day, Nasruddin ＿＿＿＿＿＿ guests for supper, so ＿＿＿＿＿＿ some ＿＿＿＿＿＿ meat for his wife ＿＿＿＿＿＿. etc.

8 REFORMULATION

a) Listen to your teacher read you this story twice. Make notes as you listen. Then rewrite the story in your own words.

b) Write a new version of the story by changing the order of events.

e.g. When his wife told Nasruddin that the cat had eaten the meat, he called for some scales. The cat weighed exactly three pounds. This all happened when . . . In the end Nasruddin said to his wife, 'If . . .'

c) Try to rewrite the story as a limerick.

e.g. The mulla's old wife was a glutton.
    She ate up the whole of the mutton.
    When she blamed the poor cat

The old man smelt a rat –
For it weighed the same weight as the mutton.

9 INTERPRETATION
a) Does this remind you of any other stories or fables?
b) Can you think of what might have happened as a continuation to
   this story?
   e.g. the Mulla's revenge on his wife
        the reactions of his friends
        what his wife said to extricate herself from the situation etc.
c) Imagine you are a journalist sent to interview Nasruddin, his wife
   and his guests so that you can write a newspaper article. Draw
   up a list of the questions you would want to ask each of them.
d) Fables usually end with a moral. Write a moral which sums up
   the lesson conveyed by this fable.

10 CREATING TEXT
Retell the story in a slightly different way. Instead of meat, use
'wine'.
   e.g. One day Nasruddin was expecting some guests to play
        cards, so he bought some wine to offer them. When they
        came his wife served them with water . . .

11 ANALYSIS
There are three points in the story where the reader has to make
connections for her/himself: after 'eaten it herself', after 'three
pounds of it', and after 'happened to the cat'. Write what you
think might have been written to make clear the connection.
   e.g. After some time Nasruddin began to get worried. He could
        not understand why no meat had been served . . .

12 PROJECT WORK
In groups, find another fable with a 'twist' in the ending, either
from this section or from elsewhere. Decide how to dramatize
the fable. After careful rehearsal perform your fable for the rest
of the class.

Some further ideas

Before choosing a text for detailed treatment, ask students to do
some activities involving an overview of all the texts. For example:
a) Skim through all the texts in this section and choose one which

you think you would like to read in detail. Read it carefully and
make notes on it. Then retell the story to a partner using your
notes to help you.
b) Look at all the stories. Are there any which are similar in any
way? (e.g. 8 and 9 or 3 and 15)
Activities which work well with the Nasruddin stories include:
2 Reduction, 6 Comparison/contrast, 7 Reconstruction, 8 Reformulation, 9 Interpretation.

Nasruddin stories

1 *Up in the Air*
'This is the pilot speaking,' came the announcement. 'We have
developed trouble in one of our engines. Please do not worry.
We will fly on the remaining three engines. This will mean we
will arrive five minutes later than scheduled.' Nasruddin tried to
calm down some of the other passengers. 'After all, what difference does five minutes make?' he said.

Shortly afterwards however, the pilot's voice came through
again. 'One of the other engines has also developed a fault. Please
remain calm. We can fly on two engines but it will mean we will
arrive half an hour late.' Nasruddin again spoke to the nervous
passengers to reassure them. 'Half an hour is nothing,' he said.
'After all, it's better than walking.'

A little later the pilot again spoke over the intercom system. 'I
am very sorry to tell you that our third engine has failed. However, there is no problem. We will fly on with the remaining
engine. This will, however, mean our arrival will be delayed by
over an hour.'

Nasruddin again spoke to the passengers.

'I only hope the last engine doesn't develop trouble. If it does,
we could be up here for ever!'

2 *How Old?*
The museum guide was showing a party of tourists round.

'This tomb is six thousand years old,' he announced.

'Excuse me,' said Nasruddin, 'but I think it is six thousand and
four years old.'

The tourists were very surprised. The guide was somewhat
upset but said nothing. In another room the guide told the group,
'This pot is three thousand years old.'

'Three thousand and four years old,' interrupted Nasruddin.

The guide was now getting angry. 'What makes you so sure?' he asked. 'How do you know the date so precisely?'

Nasruddin smiled and said, 'It's very easy really. When I came here four years ago you said the pot was three thousand years old.'

3 Boiled Eggs

When Abdul went to the restaurant, he ordered a plate of boiled eggs. When the bill came, it was for five gold pieces. Abdul called the restaurant owner over and complained that the bill was exorbitant.

'Oh no, it isn't,' said the owner. 'If I'd kept those eggs, they would have hatched into chickens. And those chickens would have laid eggs and hatched into more chickens. And they would have laid eggs in their turn. So if I hadn't sold those eggs to you, I would have had thousands more chickens – and eggs. So five gold pieces is not at all unreasonable.'

Abdul was unconvinced and decided to take his case to Nasruddin, who was the local magistrate.

Nasruddin heard the arguments on both sides. He first ordered some corn to be brought to the courtroom. He then boiled the corn. When it had cooled, he planted it in the garden.

'Why are you doing that?' asked Abdul.

'I'm planting corn so that it will grow and produce more corn,' replied Nasruddin.

'But boiled corn can't grow!' exclaimed the restaurant owner.

'Precisely,' said Nasruddin. 'So return the gold pieces to Abdul.'

4 What Problem?

Nasruddin was having problems with his memory so he went to see a psychiatrist.

'What's the problem?' asked the shrink.

'Well, it's just that I can't remember anything.'

'When did this problem start?' asked the psychiatrist.

'What problem?' said Nasruddin.

5 A Question of Time

There was once a bored and tyrannical Sultan. One day he shouted at his courtiers, 'Unless someone does something to entertain me, I'll cut all your heads off!'

Nasruddin spoke up.

'Oh mighty Sultan, I can do something to entertain you.'

'What is it?' asked the Sultan.

'I can teach a monkey to read and write,' said Nasruddin.

'Do it then,' said the Sultan. 'But, if you fail I'll execute you.'

'There's only one thing,' said Nasruddin. 'It will take ten years.'

'All right,' said the Sultan, 'I'll give you the ten years.'

When everyone had left the court, they gathered round Nasruddin.

'Can you really teach a monkey to read and write?' asked one of them.

'Of course I can't,' replied Nasruddin.

'So why did you promise to do it?' asked another.

'Easy,' said Nasruddin. 'The Sultan is eighty years old, and I am eighty-five. We'll both have other things on our minds in ten years' time!'

6 *Bad News and Good News*

Nasruddin was sitting in a coffee house in Shiraz when a stranger came in and sat at his table. He noticed a man on the other side of the room crying and tearing his hair. 'Why is he so upset?' asked the stranger.

'Because I have just come from his home town and told him that all his camel fodder has been destroyed in a fire.'

'How terrible!' said the stranger. 'It must have been difficult for you to tell him such bad news.'

'It's not so bad,' said Nasruddin, 'as I shall soon tell him the good news. The day before the fire, his camels died of a disease, so he won't be needing the fodder after all.'

7 *Questions Answered*

Nasruddin was in bad need of money, so he set up a table and put a sign up which said:

ANY TWO QUESTIONS ON ANY SUBJECT ANSWERED FOR 10 DOLLARS.

The first man to come along paid his money and asked, 'Isn't ten dollars rather a lot for two questions?'

'It certainly is,' said Nasruddin, 'and what is your second question?'

8 *What a Chopper!*

One day Nasruddin applied for a job as a woodcutter.

'You don't look strong enough to me,' said the head forester, 'but I'll give you a chance. See that plantation over there? Go and chop down as many trees as you can.'

Three days later Nasruddin came back to the head forester, who asked him, 'How many trees have you chopped down?'

'All of them,' said Nasruddin.

And it was true. Not a tree was left standing. Normally, a whole team of men would have been needed. The head forester was amazed.

'Where did you learn to chop down trees so fast?' he asked.

'In the Sahara desert,' said Nasruddin.

'But there are no trees in the Sahara desert,' said the forester.

'Not *now*, there aren't,' replied Nasruddin.

9 *No Tigers*

One of his neighbours found Nasruddin scattering crumbs all around his house.

'Why are you doing that?' he asked.

'I'm keeping the tigers away,' replied Nasruddin.

'But there aren't any tigers round here,' said the neighbour.

'That's right,' said Nasruddin. 'You can see how effective it is.'

10 *What is Truth?*

One day there was a powerful king who decided he would force his people to be truthful.

At the entrance to his kingdom there was a bridge and on the bridge he built a gallows. He put up a notice which announced, 'Everyone who enters the kingdom will be questioned. If he tells the truth, he will be allowed to come in. If he lies, he will be hanged.'

Nasruddin was the first to come forward. The guard stopped him and said, 'What are you going to do?'

'I am on my way to be hanged,' replied Nasruddin.

'I don't believe you!'

'In that case, if I have told a lie hang me,' said Nasruddin with a smile.

'But, but, but if I hang you for telling a lie, I will make what you said come true!' said the guard, totally confused.

'That's right,' said Nasruddin, 'so what *is* the truth?'

11 *Candle-power*

One day Nasruddin made a bet with some friends that he could stay all night on a mountain-top nearby and survive the ice and snow till morning.

He took a book with him and a candle to read by and spent
the coldest night he could remember on the mountain-top. In
the morning, frozen to the bone, he came down and asked for
the bet to be paid.

'Wait a minute,' said one of his friends, 'didn't you take anything to keep you warm? That would be cheating.'

'No,' said Nasruddin.

'What about a candle?' said another.

'Oh yes, I had a candle to read my book by.'

'Sorry – you cheated, we're not going to pay,' said his friends.
Nasruddin said nothing and went home.

A few months later, he invited his friends to a special supper.
Everyone sat down and waited for the food to arrive. An hour
went by, then two, then three. Finally one of them asked Nasruddin where the food was.

'Perhaps we'd better go to the kitchen and see what's happening,' said Nasruddin.

When they got there, they found an enormous cauldron of
water under which a candle was burning.

'That's funny,' said Nasruddin. 'I can't understand why it's
not ready yet. I put it on last night.'

12 *Do You Know or Don't You?*

People were always trying to play jokes on Nasruddin. One day
the villagers invited him to give a sermon in their mosque to
make a fool of him.

When he arrived in the mosque he went to the pulpit and said:
'Do you people know what I am going to talk to you about?'

'No, we don't,' the congregation replied.

'Then how can I talk to people as ignorant as you. You're
wasting my time.' And he came down from the pulpit and went
straight home.

The leaders went back to visit him and pleaded with him to
preach to them the following Friday instead.

Again Nasruddin asked the same question but this time the
villagers all answered, 'Yes, we do.'

'So why do you need me to talk to you at all?' asked Nasruddin
scornfully, and he left the mosque and went home again.

The villagers begged him to come back again the following
Friday. Eventually he agreed.

Again he asked the same question. This time the villagers
replied, 'Some of us do and some of us don't.'

'In that case,' said Nasruddin, 'let the ones who know tell the ones who don't!' And he went home yet again.

13 No Need for a Net

The King of the country needed to find a modest, humble man who could be made a judge. So he sent a confidential delegation round the country looking for such a man.

Nasruddin got to hear of this and when the delegation came, pretending to be merchants, they found him sitting with a fishing-net round his shoulders.

'Why are you wearing that net?' they asked.

'I wear it to remind me of my lowly origins; I was born into a fisherman's family,' replied Nasruddin.

The delegation were so impressed that they recommended Nasruddin for the job of judge and he was appointed soon afterwards.

About a year later one of the members of the delegation happened to visit the court-house where Nasruddin was hearing cases.

'Why aren't you wearing your net any more?' he asked.

'Well, now I've caught the fish, I don't need the net, do I?' replied Nasruddin.

14 Getting Up is Good for You

One day Nasruddin's father told him, 'You should always get up very early in the morning.'

'Why is that, Father?' asked Nasruddin.

'Well, for example, once when I went for a walk early in the morning I found a bag of money lying in the road.'

'But perhaps it was lost the previous night?' suggested Nasruddin.

'No, no,' said his father, 'I did not see it there the night before.'

'Well in that case getting up early can't be good for everyone,' said Nasruddin. 'The man who lost the money must have been up even earlier than you were.'

15 Duck Soup

One of Nasruddin's country cousins came to visit him. The man brought him a duck as a present and Nasruddin had it cooked and had it for supper with his cousin.

Some weeks later another visitor arrived. 'I am a friend of the man who brought you the duck,' he said.

Nasruddin invited him to supper; fed him and sent him on his way the next morning.

Over the next few weeks this happened six or seven times. Nasruddin began to feel as if he was running a free restaurant.

Eventually he lost his patience. The next time a visitor came who announced that he was 'a friend of the man who brought you the duck', Nasruddin invited him to sit down and asked his wife to bring in the soup.

The visitor tasted it but it had no flavour at all. In fact it tasted just like warm water.

'Excuse me,' said the guest, 'but can you tell me what kind of soup this is?'

'Of course,' said Nasruddin. 'That is the soup of the soup of the soup of the soup of the duck.'

Most of the short essays collected here were originally written to be broadcast. They are therefore fairly informal in style and were written for broadcast within strict time-limits (2–3 minutes air time).

The Sample Text:
Serious Travel or 'My Son, the Conference Delegate!'
I used to like organizing conferences, because I fancied myself as a 'fixer'. I had low tastes. I like being in the inner circle, in the know, among those who mattered, lording it over the suckers, who sat in the back rows.

It was quite deplorable, and unspeakably vulgar, and I am thankful I grew out of it before I corrupted myself completely. As I became more secure, I didn't need such false reassurance.

I still go to conferences sometimes as a speaker. But as soon as I decently can, I retire to the back rows I once despised. There I suck sweets, chew gum, and exchange ribald remarks with other delegates and observers. It's much more fun.

Wisdom rarely comes from a keynote address or from any platform exhortation – they are too ponderous. It surfaces in corridors, over cups of tea, and at the conference bar. Now I no longer want to manage people, I enjoy them instead!

I EXPANSION
Write a paragraph which could introduce the topic, another to insert after the second paragraph and one which could serve as a kind of conclusion.
e.g. • *introduction*: I suppose most people have been to a conference at one time or another. They are usually busy affairs with everyone rushing . . .
   • *after second paragraph*: Looking back I can see that my behaviour was extraordinary and it is hard to believe I was the same person . . .
   • *conclusion*: And do you know what? Not only do I enjoy myself more these days but . . .

2 REDUCTION

Cut out all unnecessary words and phrases to make the text about half its present length.

e.g. I used to like organizing conferences.

I liked being among those who mattered.

It was deplorable and I am thankful I grew out of it . . .

Discuss your proposed cuts in a whole-class session with your teacher.

3 MEDIA TRANSFER

a) Change this from an essay into an interview with a media journalist. The interview should contain all the main information from the text.

e.g. Q. Now, I understand that you used to be a great conferencer-goer. Is that right?

A. Oh yes. But not only a conference-goer. I used to like organizing conferences, too.

Q. Used to?

A. Oh yes. I grew out of it thank goodness . . .

b) Copy out the whole text *as if* it was a poem. That is, you must decide on where the 'lines' end.

e.g. I used to like organizing conferences

Because I fancied myself

As a 'fixer'.

I had low tastes.

I liked being in the inner circle,

In the know,

Among those who mattered . . .

If you read it aloud as a poem, does it sound like a poem?

4 MATCHING

a) Choose the title which best matches the text:
  • Pride Comes before a Fall
  • Worm's-eye View
  • Where the Wisdom Is
  • Down from the Platform
  • Changing Places
  • From the Back Row

b) Look at the section on diary entries (p. 44). Check the entries by Lord Reith (p. 48) and Pepys (p. 48). Which of them best matches the sense of this text?

5 SELECTION/RANKING

a) Choose the proverb or saying which best approximates to the meaning of the text and put the others in order from most to least like the text.
   - Empty vessels make most noise.
   - Distance lends enchantment to the view.
   - Fine clothes do not make a gentleman.
   - There is always room at the top. (Daniel Webster)
   - Every arrow that flies feels the attraction of earth. (Walter Ralegh)
   - Ambition often puts men upon doing the meanest offices; so climbing is performed in the same position with creeping. (Jonathan Swift)
   - All that glitters is not gold.

b) Select the sentences below which you think are *not* true about the text.
   i) The writer enjoys himself more these days.
   ii) He used to be a very confident person.
   iii) He used to have good taste.
   iv) He used to enjoy the feeling of power.
   v) Good ideas do not usually arise in informal situations.
   vi) He is a nicer person now than he was before.
   vii) He used to despise ordinary people.
   viii) He regrets giving up his role as conference organizer.

6 COMPARISON/CONTRAST

Compare the following poem with the text:

I am now a nobody
Who was once a somebody.
Being a somebody was nice
At the time
But there was a price
For the climb.

So I left the front row
And settled at the back.
People here are nice you know
And somehow have the knack
Of talking better sense
Than all those proudly puffing gents.

If you can stop listening to yourself
And start listening to others,
It's remarkable what is revealed
Which self-importance smothers.
    A.M.

What similarities can you find between the two pieces? And what differences? Make two columns and enter in the similarities and differences.

e.g.

Similarities	*Differences*
Both deal with ambition, self-importance etc.	The prose has very specific details, the poem is more general.
Both imply or state that there is a 'price for glory'. etc.	In the poem, the writer has 'opted out' completely. In the prose text the writer still speaks at conferences etc.

7 RECONSTRUCTION

a) These four paragraphs are in the wrong order. Put them back into an order which makes sense for you.

  i)   I still go to conferences . . . fun.

  ii)   It was quite deplorable . . . reassurance.

  iii) Wisdom rarely comes . . . enjoy them instead.

  iv) I used to like organizing . . . back rows.

b) These *five* paragraphs are in the wrong order.

  i)   It was quite deplorable, and unspeakably vulgar, and I am thankful I grew out of it before I corrupted myself completely. As I became more secure, I didn't need such false reassurance.

  ii)   I used to like organizing conferences, because I fancied myself as a 'fixer'. I had low tastes. I liked being in the inner circle, in the know, among those who mattered, lording it over the suckers, who sat in the back rows.

  iii) I was after all still very well known. But getting involved with the details of organization was increasingly uncongenial to me. In any case, I was in so much demand as a speaker that I had no time for organizational work.

  iv) I still go to conferences sometimes as a speaker. But as soon as I decently can, I retire to the back rows I once despised. There I suck sweets, chew gum, and exchange ribald remarks with other delegates and observers. It's much more fun.

v)   Wisdom rarely comes from a keynote address or from any platform exhortation – they are too ponderous. It surfaces in corridors, over cups of tea, and at the conference bar. Now I no longer want to manage people, I enjoy them instead!

One of the five paragraphs does not fit, so you will have to decide which it is and remove it.

8 REFORMULATION

Rewrite the text, expressing the opposite viewpoint: that being involved in managing conferences, and other people, is very important to you; you would not consider taking a back seat with all those 'ordinary' people.

9 INTERPRETATION

a) Consider these two statements. Do you agree with them? Can you think of examples to illustrate them?
   • All power corrupts. Absolute power corrupts absolutely.
   • It takes a lot of courage to be a nobody.
b) Can you think of anyone you know (or have heard of) who voluntarily decided to take 'a back seat' after being 'in the driving seat'?
c) What questions would you want to ask the writer so as to get a more complete picture of his decision and the reasons for it? Draw up a list as if you were going to interview him.

10 CREATING TEXT

a) Imagine that you are sitting with the writer in the back row at a conference. Write a sketch of the conversation you have. (For example, you will probably pass comments on the speaker's voice or speech mannerisms, his views and whether or not you agree with them, his past history, his appearance etc. You may also tell each other jokes, talk about other things that you are looking forward to etc.) When you have finished perform your sketch for another pair.
b) Select up to twelve 'chunks' from the text. (A 'chunk' may be anything from a word up to a short sentence.)
   e.g. I fancied myself/lording it over the suckers/It's much more fun/vulgar/etc.

Then work with a partner to combine these into a poem (which does *not* have to be a repetition of the message of the text).

11 ANALYSIS

a) Look at the tenses used in the text. What do you notice about those in the first and second paragraphs and in the third and fourth paragraphs? Is the function of the tense used in the last paragraph the same as that in the third?

b) Make a list of all the adjectives in the text. Divide them into those with a positive feeling, those with a negative feeling and those which are neutral. How many of the adjectives can also be used as nouns?

c) Notice how the writer indicates the changes in his attitudes: I used to . . ., I still . . ., I no longer . . .

12 PROJECT WORK

In groups, prepare a questionnaire which will probe people's attitudes to ambition and success. Then use it to get answers from as many different people as you can. Tabulate your results and present them to the rest of the class. They can then be put on the class notice-board.

Some further ideas

It may be a good idea to familiarize students with all the texts in this section in advance. For example:

a) Divide the class into groups. Give each group a different text to read as homework preparation. In the next lesson each group nominates a spokesperson to give a summary of the ideas and content of the group's text.

b) Each group prepares questions which they would like to have answered on a particular text. Groups then exchange texts and questions and attempt to answer the questions they have received.

The essays on reflections on life work especially well with the following activities:

2 Reduction, 3 Media transfer, 5 Selection/ranking, 6 Comparison/contrast, 8 Reformulation, 11 Analysis.

Short essays – reflections on life

1 *Life is a Moving Staircase*

Even if we stand still in space, we journey through time. Life is an escalator like those in stores and underground stations. We move on, though we do nothing.

The same things surround us, but we see them always from

new perspectives. I live once again with my mother and aunt in a suburban house – we were in the same situation fifty years ago. But now our roles are reversed, and I am the caring adult. There is a lot to think about.

There is a lot to ponder in the fabric of ordinary life, in the familiar, routine, and unremarkable happenings of an ordinary day. At first I was too romantic and snobbish to see it. Now, I know I do not only have to read scriptures, I also have to decipher the scripture that is unfolding around me.

 Rabbi Lionel Blue

2 *Last Month We Closed a Factory*

Last month we Closed a factory.

When I say 'we' I mean the small business of which I am a part-time Director.

I don't suppose that these decisions are ever taken lightly, and this one certainly wasn't. But we had to face the facts: the factory had been losing money for two years and we could not let it bleed the rest of the business to death.

The business logic was clear. The human logic was just awful. How do you explain to people who have been working harder than ever, and producing more than ever before, that it was all useless – the stuff still sold at a loss, the more they made the more we lost. Economics can be a baffling science.

We listened to men, and women, telling us what it would be like to lose their jobs in an area where there were no new jobs. Many would never have a paid job again and it wouldn't be their fault. I felt like a judge passing sentence on the innocent.

Whose fault *was* it? Some said it was ours for not keeping them in jobs until all the money ran out, just in case things turned up. But we saw, all too clearly, that if we didn't close that factory now the whole lot would go. Isn't it better that some should go so that others might live? Not if it's you that goes, it isn't. It may be glorious to die for one's country but it isn't yet glorious to be made redundant for your firm. Should it be?

Some knew it was no one's fault. Nothing lasts for ever. New technology, or new habits, put paid to many things we took for granted. The candles I went to bed with every night when I was a boy in the depths of the country are now, for us, kept for special occasions. The electric light is easier for us but it was tough on the candlemakers. Death and then new life, in business as in nature. It's OK if it's nature and winter is followed by spring but it's tougher in business when only winter is on offer, and spring is in other parts of the country and for other skills.

'Get on your bike then,' the man said, but did he know that only ten per cent of the unemployed have bikes?

Some blamed the system. 'If it all belonged to everyone then everyone could have jobs,' they said. Not in that plant they couldn't, and not at those wages. You can change the owners but that doesn't change the cost of the product.

Some accused us of playing God. We were, they thought, sitting in that peculiar kind of heaven called a Board Room disposing of people's lives to suit our own grand design. Playing God? It didn't feel like that at all, unfortunately, at least not my kind of god.

My god would have found a way to give *each individual* the glimpse of new life in this kind of death and the means to grasp that life. My god would have found some light to shine on each person's darkness, some way of giving new meaning to each life, some way of discovering new talents in each of them and pushing them towards new opportunities. My god would have made them feel sure that they lived on, even when the factory died.

We did our best to do all this but I'm afraid it won't be enough for many at that plant, and many won't even believe we meant it. After all, institutions, no matter how well-intentioned, no matter who owns them or runs them, are no match for God. Perhaps no one should expect them to be.

Charles Handy

3 *Group-think*

Last week I went to stay with my mother-in-law. Now mothers-in-law aren't for staying with in the myth, but actually I greatly enjoy my time there. Not only does she ply me with excellent food and drink but I get to read her newspapers! That provides me with a very different view of Britain from the one which I normally get over breakfast. How strange to find that not everyone is arguing rationally about the Anglo-Irish agreement, economic forecasts or the latest business merger. What odd interests other people have!

The truth is that it's very good for me to be bereft of my normal newspapers. I have to start to think for myself. No pre-packaged set of opinions on the issues of the day are there to confirm my prejudice and tell me what to say. My comfort-zone removed. We are all quite good, I guess, at creating these comfort-zones – not just newspapers, but friends who think like us. It's what makes life predictable.

In the jargon of my profession it is called group-think, a state of affairs in which all around are of a common mind so that no one notices that the emperor is actually naked, or at least would never presume to say so. I shall always remember the fascinating research studies of the groups where all but one of the members are briefed beforehand to say that what is clearly the shorter of two lines seems to them to be the longer one, with the result that the one unbriefed member begins to doubt the evidence of his own eyes and will, in fact, usually agree with the majority!

It sounds bizarre. But it happens. I can think of too many times when I've nodded my head for the sake of a quiet life, when I've let myself be argued into agreeing to something which I know is wrong. A decent humility, you might say, or a respect for others. Too often it's just cowardice, or laziness – the comfort of group-think. Organizations are rife with group-think. They not only read the same newspapers, they wear the same clothes, tell the same jokes. They even glory in it, calling it 'shared values'. Shared values are great, of course, if the values are great.

But those shared values can also lull you into a sort of moral anaesthesia, where you find yourself agreeing too readily that the obvious way to deal with the fall in profits is to amputate a bit of the organization, that it's OK to fantasize your expenses because it's 'the unwritten law of the firm', that you must cut yourself in on the action because 'everyone expects it'. Cocooned by like-minds we can drift into a moral swamp like the man who was amazed to find himself jailed for being what he thought was just a clever businessman.

Truth actually is important, I reckon; being true to oneself, that is. Living a lie does not feel good and organizations which lie to themselves come to a distressingly predictable end. Best to remember the psalmist who reckoned heaven was for him 'who doeth the thing which is right and speaketh the truth from his heart', or to go with George Orwell who said that even if you are in a minority of one you aren't necessarily mad.

'Know yourself,' said the Greeks. 'Be yourself,' I would add. It may not be comfortable. It has to be better.

Charles Handy

4 *Not So Funny After All*

I once had a secretary, when I worked in London, who had a

special working arrangement; as she was a married woman with exceptional responsibilities at home, an invalid husband or mother, I forget which, she used to arrive in the office at ten o'clock and left at four. As my work consisted very largely in interviewing, discussion, committee meetings and visiting other organizations, I was seldom able to dictate anything between ten and four. I used to catch an early train to Charing Cross, so as to be in the office by eight o'clock and I wrote all my correspondence in long-hand. My secretary typed the letters during the day, and I signed them just before she left. Of course she answered the telephone and kept my list of appointments, but otherwise she couldn't do much for me; but she was pretty and occasionally brought flowers to relieve the gloom of an uninspiring office. I may be doing her an injustice, but I had the impression that she went to the hair-dresser almost every day, so there was seldom time at midday to dictate anything.

One day I attended a demonstration of a machine into which one dictated one's letters, which could later be typed. After the demonstration I asked if the machine ever went to the hair-dresser. The answer was 'No'. I told my secretary about the demonstration and said that the machine had one significant advantage: the demonstrater had assured me that it never went to the hair-dresser. 'No,' she said, 'and it never laughs at your jokes either.'

Lionel Billows

5 The One That Got Away

She was sitting in the front row of one of my evening classes at a medium-sized town in central Anatolia. She looked as if she might be about 18 or 19; she answered up well and was obviously intelligent. She knew more English than most of the rest. After the class I asked her if she was a school-girl.

'No,' she said, she had left school. My stay for a month in this shabby town was an attempt to help the adult education movement, so school-boys and girls were not allowed. They might know more than the grown-ups and make them feel shy and nervous.

The next day I was asked to teach the top class in the secondary school. There she was, looking rather self-conscious, in the back row. Like the others she was wearing the black overall with a white collar which was the school uniform and her hair was tied back modestly, unlike the more fashionable look she had managed the night before.

The next evening, when she came to the class, I asked severely: 'Why did you say you had left school? You know school-girls are not allowed in these classes. You told me a deliberate lie.'

'Yes, I know,' she answered, quite unrepentant, 'and so would you, if you badly wanted to get into a class like this and there was no other chance.'

I laughed and let her stay, but made her promise to be very grown-up. I didn't regret it, she learnt well and behaved modestly. She came to be my chief memory of that month.

A year later I visited the town again and met her father in the street. He said she had begun to study architecture in Istanbul. He gave me her address and asked me to look her up. I was on my way to Istanbul anyway and would have done so, but I caught a bad cold, so that a colleague and his wife fetched me from my hotel and nursed me till I was well enough to go back to Ankara. So I never saw her again and lost her address. Perhaps I was afraid of falling in love with her.

Lionel Billows

6 *Nicotine Nonsense*

Another facility which I find I have developed, as a consequence of working in a publicity department, is the ability to feel sympathy with the unfortunate wretches who have to live by recommending products which they know are useless or even harmful. So it is not without a certain wicked glee, which the Germans call *schadenfreude*, that I observe the contortions of the people who try to persuade us to poison ourselves with nicotine and other noxious substances which are contained in cigarette smoke.

They claim that the cigarette they are paid to recommend contains less of these harmful substances, but has more taste than before. The first of these assertions may be true and is probably verifiable by chemical analysis, but the second is almost impossible to prove and may well not be true. In any case tastes in taste are frequently different and therefore not really predictable. So the sole claim to recommend the cigarette, which is impartially verifiable is, that it is less poisonous than its poisonous predecessors. This is faint praise indeed.

In the thirties there was a cigarette which many people thought gave them sore throats and more and more complaints came in to the manufacturer. It is clear to most people that any cigarette can cause sore throats, so the manufacturer, or rather his publicity chief, who happened to be a friend or brother-in-law of a colleague of mine, was perfectly justified in the steps he took. The slogan from then on was printed on every packet 'Specially made for sore throats', and the complaints, from that moment, ceased.

Lionel Billows

7 *The Descent of Mam*

The Mam people, known in their own language as 'the Children of the Sun', are among the last surviving descendants of the Maya. They live beyond the mist in the Cuchumatan mountains of eastern Guatemala, and it was their remoteness that saved them from decimation by the invading Spaniards. They are still a long way from anywhere: the village of Todos Santos is only 30 miles from the region's main city, Huehuetenango, but it is a rough two-hour ride in a jeep.

The Mam live in the old way. They share their adobe houses with their pet chickens and turkeys, and cultivate maize and kidney beans which entwine together as they grow. Many of the men do seasonal work in farms on the coast to bring in a little cash. In the village each family weaves its own clothes and has its own sauna, a hut where water is thrown on heated stones to produce steam, the ancient bathing system of the Maya.

It sounds a pleasant enough existence, but in today's world such idylls are fragile. In 1988, the mayor of Huehuetenango decided to teach the Mam the error of their ways. Social scientists declared that only 27 per cent of Mam were literate, that many of their animals were diseased, and that the Mam themselves were undernourished. To help them raise their standards of living, vets from an organization called Veterinarios sin Fronteras equipped with hypodermics and bottles of pills struggled up the mountain. They instructed the Mam how better to take care of their pet chickens and turkeys and cows, so they could subsequently kill and eat them. While the Mam looked on in indignation, the vets jabbed needles into the cows and horses – but when the jabbed animals began outliving the rest, the attitude of the Mam began to change.

Soon canned foods and man-made fibres, television and Coca-Cola will follow the vets up the mountainside, and another out-post of barbarism will have fallen.

Peter Popham
The Independent Magazine, 6 March 1993

8 *Listen to the Lions*

Grimethorpe was a farming village set in rolling West Riding countryside when the Mitchell family sank its first mineshaft in 1894. By the time the pits were nationalized, fifty years later, Mitchell Main Colliery dominated the landscape. Once there were more than 2,500 miners working its seams; now there are fewer than 800, and in January there will be none. In less than a century, an industry will have come and gone, first creating a community and then erasing it, leaving behind only useless skills, empty traditions, four generations' worth of memories, and a profound sense of uncertainty that is suddenly shared across the country. Whether or not, as has been said, they were led by donkeys, the lions of Grimethorpe are on the brink of extinction.

The Independent on Sunday
1 *November 1992*

ANSWERS SECTION

1 One-line texts

p.12   4   Don't kill the goose that lays the golden eggs.

p.12   5a) Nature conservation

          5b) This is one possible order:

- Eat the egg and not the chicken.
- Live today and pay tomorrow.
- Great oaks from little acorns grow.
- Look after the pence and the pounds will look after themselves.
- Spare the rod and spoil the child.
- The proof of the pudding is in the eating.

p.13   10b) e.g.
- A rolling stone gathers no moss.
- Waste not, want not.
- Strike while the iron is hot.
- Nothing ventured, nothing gained.
- Don't put all your eggs in one basket.

p.14   11a) Imperative

          11b) The definite article is used because this gives universal meaning.

              i.e. the grape = grapes in general.

2 Haiku

p.18   1c) e.g. We started out early in the morning. We planned to cross the mountains and go down to the valley beyond. It was a hard climb but eventually we got to the top and could see the river below.

              Finally we got to the river. What a relief it was to plunge our feet into it – so refreshing. James had picked some plums on the way down. They tasted delicious! But our hearts sank when we looked at the long climb back up the mountain.

              It was almost dark by the time we got back to the camp and everyone was so exhausted that we all went straight to bed.

p.19   4a) Any of these could fit.

          4b) Here are some possibilities:
               autumn wind –
               mountain's shadow
               wavers
                    Issa

               summer night:
               we turn out all the lights
               to hear the rain
                    Peggy Willis Lyles

               august heat;
               the coolness of eggs
               in a blue crock
                    Emily Romano

p.19   5b) The best order is the one they are in already.

3 Mini-texts

p.27   4c) e.g. A letter for him . . .
                    You came. You were late . . .

p.27   5a) Any of them could be used but perhaps 'Never' and
               'Silence' are especially appropriate.

p.29   11a) The past simple tense is used throughout except for the
               present simple use of 'remember'.

          11b) First four sentences: He
               Fifth sentence: We
               Sixth sentence: I
               Last sentence: It
               There seems to be a pattern of movement from 'he' to
               the togetherness of 'we', then to the isolation of 'I' and
               the final impersonality of 'it'.

4 Epitaphs

p.36   4a) ii) and iii) match best.

          4b) The closest are 'Jemmy Wyatt' (no. 14) and 'Blown
               Upward' (no. 2).

p.36   5a) The best order is ii), iii), i).

p.37   9b) It was obviously written after the death took place. And
               it could not have been written by the 'I' (who is dead!).

          9c) It does not say what caused death.

p.38   11a) Grim Death *took me* . . . = I died.
        11b) e.g. 'John Bunn' (no. 1), 'Catherine Stone' (no.19),
             'Jane Key' (no. 21).

5 Diary entries

p.45   4a) ii) is the only possibility.
        4b) Possibly 'A stick has two ends.'
p.45   5a) A probable order would be:
            • Like Son, Like Father
            • Never Look Back
            • The Damning Diary
            • Understanding Who?
            but others are possible.
        5b) iii), i), ii).
p.46   8a) The three words to change are:
            appalled, vulgarity, priggishness.
p.47   9b) father/son

6 Short poems

p.56   1c) *long* grey beards . . .
            the *old* bald . . .
            buzzing bees . . .
            electrons, *protons*, gases . . .
            Old *style* nebulae . . .
            Each *blindfold* specialist . . .
            professional *sounding* oaf . . .
            his *dried-up* little . . .
            the *universal* loaf!
p.57   4a) The two best possibilities are 'Whose Truth?' and 'Food
            for Thought'. 'Bread and Circuses' is not acceptable.
        4b) e.g. *one-liners*: Erudition (n) Dust shaken out of a book
                 into an empty skull.
                 I am Right: You are Wrong.
                 Nasruddin stories: 2, 12
                 short essays: Serious Travel . . . (Sample Text)
p.58   5   a), b), d), c).
p.61   9b) Someone who is familiar with conferences of specialists
            and is sceptical about them. Perhaps a journalist.
        9c) 'Miniature' could refer to this snapshot of a conference
            (a miniature is a small picture or portrait). It could

also refer to the tiny crumbs of knowledge which each specialist possesses. It could also refer to the specialists themselves: miniature people with no breadth of vision.

9e) ironic, sarcastic, cynical, sceptical, mocking etc.

p.61   11a) Present simple. This is used as the so-called 'historic present' to make the event more vivid, as if it were happening *now*. The past tense would make it less immediate.

11b) The rhyme scheme is regular:
a b a b   c d c d

11c) Alliteration: <u>g</u>ases, <u>G</u>od
<u>n</u>ebulae, <u>n</u>ew <u>fl</u>eas
<u>d</u>ry-as-<u>d</u>ust
<u>c</u>rumb of <u>c</u>rust/And <u>c</u>ries . . .

11d) Assonance: nebul<u>ae</u>, new <u>fl</u>eas
cr<u>u</u>mb of cr<u>u</u>st
H<u>o</u>lds . . . Beh<u>o</u>ld the l<u>oa</u>f!

7 Prayers

p.70   4   Those which fit best are:
b), a), e).

p.70   5a) b), a), e), c), d), f)

5b) Almost any order could be justified.
i), ii), iii) is preferable.
ii), i), iii) also plausible.

p.71   9a) The author was only thirty-seven when she died – so the prayer was probably not answered.

p.71   11a) The only words repeated are:
work, till, my and *life.*

8 Programme notes

p.78   1   *topical* science, *highly critical* report, *qualified* boffins, *company* boardrooms, *commercial* companies, *management* positions, *obvious* assumption, *industrial* research, *severely* critical, *yawning* divide, *current* British education, *strong* plea, *British* industry.

p.79   4   Any of these could be chosen;
b) and d) are preferable.

9 Mini-sagas

p.87   1b) e.g. *Before the text*:
Peter and Gill had met when they were at university.
It was love at first sight. After a whirlwind romance
they married in the year they both graduated. He
became a successful research scientist. She continued
her work as a fashion designer.
After the text:
After that they gradually drifted apart. He could no
longer share his thoughts with her. And she felt an
obscure guilt at what she had done. One day in May,
she told him she would be leaving him for a new life
in Canada.

p.91   11b) • union – bond
• prised open – forced open
• ashamed – guilty
• shared – jointly owned
• space – area

10 Short newspaper articles

p.96   1a) *Blithely* waving, *illegally* speeding, *abruptly* stopped,
hurtling *headlong*, *completely* level, *immediately*
responded, *suggestively* dangling, pull over *immediately*,
persuasively explained, *helpfully* provided.

p.96   2   . . . to indicate the urgency of their mission . . .
. . . according to a report in *The Lancet*.
. . . to an emergency case . . .
. . . in the outside lane.
. . . there was a happy ending:
. . . for the rest of their journey.

p.97   4   Presentation C

p.97   5a) • More haste, less speed.
• There's a time and place for everything.
• Time and tide wait for no man.
• The Future is something which everyone reaches at
the rate of 60 minutes an hour, whatever he does,
whoever he is.
• He who hesitates is lost.
• A stitch in time saves nine.

5b) Best: Fast Aid!
        Least: Emergency Stop
p.100 11a) 'just this' = 'waving a stethoscope while speeding'
        11b) doctors = medics
        police = uniformed occupants
        emergency case = urgency of their mission
        speeding = hurtling
        waving = dangling

11 Nasruddin stories

p.107 1b) One day Nasruddin was *anxiously* expecting some
        guests for supper, so he *carefully* bought some goat's
        meat for his wife to cook. When the guests had arrived,
        his wife *obediently* served lots of vegetable dishes but no
        meat – she had already *greedily* eaten it herself. 'Where's
        the meat?' inquired Nasruddin *nonchalantly*. 'The cat ate
        it – all three pounds of it,' replied his wife *innocently*.
        Nasruddin *solemnly* called for some scales, then *carefully*
        weighed the cat . . .
p.108 4 You can't have your cake and eat it, *or* You can't have
        it both ways.
p.108 5 'Scapegoat', meaning blaming someone else for your
        own misdeeds, is a clever title but probably 'Scales of
        Justice' or 'Vanishing Trick' would make better titles.
        Here is a possible order:
        • Scales of Justice
        • Vanishing Trick
        • Scapegoat
        • A Weighty Matter
        • Where's It Gone?
        • The Meat of the Argument
        • The Goat, the Cat and the Wife

12 Short essays – reflections on life

p.119 4a) The best matches are:
        'Down from the Platform', 'Changing Places' or 'From
        the Back Row'.
p.120 5a) Probably the best fit is 'All that glitters is not gold'.
        • All that glitters is not gold.
        • Every arrow that flies . . .

- Distance lends enchantment to the view.
- Ambition often . . .
- Fine clothes do not make a gentleman.
- Empty vessels make most noise.
- There is always room at the top.

p.123   5b) Not true: iii), v), vii)

11a) First and second paragraphs use the past tense forms. Third and fourth use the present simple tense. But in paragraph 3 this refers to concrete activities which he engaged in. In paragraph 4 he uses it to refer to general truths.

11b)

Positive	Negative	Neutral
inner	low	keynote
back	back	platform
thankful	deplorable	conference
secure	vulgar	
ribald	false	
	ponderous	

Adjectives/Nouns

conference bar
keynote address
platform exhortation
back rows